DANGEROUS

DUSK

Aleatha Romig

New York Times, Wall Street Journal, and USA Today
bestselling author of the Consequences, Infidelity, Web of Sin,
Tangled Web, and Web of Desire series

COPYRIGHT AND LICENSE INFORMATION

or are used fictitiously, and any resemblance to any actual persons, living or dead, events, or locales is entirely coincidental.

2020 Edition License

DUSK

book #1 DANGEROUS WEB

"When your whole world is shaken from all the risks we have taken, dance with me. Dance with me into the colors of the dusk." ~ **Ben Harper.**

I've served my country, a man, and a cause. I've given my whole being while at the same time finding its true meaning. There was no way for me to know that the day I met the men who were to become my best friends, they would introduce me to the love of my life.

Fiery red hair and hypnotizing emerald eyes caught my attention.

Creamy, soft skin, a stark contrast to mine, seduced my body.

Strength, devotion, and determination stole my heart.

I am Reid Murray, and I'll kill without regret to once again dance in the dusk with my wife. This war has only begun. I won't rest until it's done.

From New York Times bestselling author Aleatha Romig comes a brand-new romantic suspense trilogy, Dangerous Web. DUSK, book #1, is set in the dangerous world of the Sparrow Webs. You do not need to read Web of Sin, Tangled Web, or Web of Desire to get caught up in this new dark-romance saga, Dangerous Web.

DUSK is book one of the *DANGEROUS WEB* trilogy that continues in *DARK* and concludes in *DAWN*.

Have you been Aleatha'd?

DEDICATION

*To everyone who has fallen in love, over and over, with different
fictional characters for different reasons during different seasons. To
everyone who has finished one book with a smile on their face saying,
"This was the best," only to open another. To every reader who has the
courage to open themselves up for more love, laughs, tears, and even
heartbreak.*

*Life, like books, keeps coming. The best thing we can do is hold on for
the ride.*

*Thank you for taking that ride, that journey with the Sparrow Webs.
Thank you for loving Sterling and Araneae, Mason/Kader and
Laurel, Patrick and Madeline, and now Reid and Lorna.*

*Please join me once again in the glass tower, with the ladies and the
men, with family of blood and of choice. Please accept your invitation
to be an integral part of the Sparrows because we are not finished.
There is more story to share.*

Hold on for more...Sparrow Webs.
Dusk—the moment at the very end of astronomical twilight, the darkest part.
Are you ready to be Aleatha'd once again?

NOTE FROM ALEATHA

Dangerous Web begins nine years after Lorna and Reid's first meeting in DANGER'S FIRST KISS, a novella that first appeared in DARK FAIRY TALES, a limited release anthology.

You do not need to read DANGER'S FIRST KISS before reading *Dangerous Web*.

If however, you would like read about their first meeting, told in a modern-day *Cinderella* themed story, please search for DARK FAIRY TALES, or after it is no longer available, DANGER'S FIRST KISS, by Aleatha, on your favorite retailer.

I hope you enjoy Reid and Lorna's dramatic romantic suspense story—*Dangerous Web*.

Thank you for reading the Sparrow Webs. You're about to read DUSK, book #1 of the final trilogy, *Dangerous Web*.

If this is your first trilogy of the Sparrow Webs, please know that there are other amazing stories in this same world ready to binge today.

Web of Sin
SECRETS (Free everywhere)
LIES
PROMISES

Tangled Web
TWISTED
OBSESSED
BOUND

Web of Desire
SPARK
FLAME
ASHES

For a complete list of my books, please go to "Books by Aleatha" following DUSK. Thank you again for falling in love with the Sparrow Web world, enjoy.

-Aleatha

DANGEROUS WEB #1

DUSK

Book #1 of the DANGEROUS WEB trilogy in SPARROW WEBS

Aleatha Romig

New York Times, Wall Street Journal, and USA Today bestselling author of the Consequences, Infidelity, and Web of Sin series

LORNA

*M*y body ached, every muscle, fiber, tendon, artery, and vein. A fire raged within me, unattended, a blaze on the verge of total devastation. And while the singe of the flames burned through my insides, I was paralyzed—helpless to escape. All around me, monstrous trees and giant structures melted under the intense heat as the blaring snap and crackle consumed my hearing. Years of work, accomplishment, and adoration burned, leaving behind a trail of ashes.

I came to my senses or maybe they came to me. An out-of-body experience as if I were trudging through deep muck, the kind of place seen on a movie or television show—a marsh or a bayou. Shadows of vegetation loomed as insects feasted on my skin. I couldn't swat them away. I had to keep moving. Each step was a struggle, each thought filled with uncertainty.

My journey knew no end, no destination. The path was as dark as a starless night. I lifted my hands to feel what I couldn't see. My temples throbbed and my heart raced as I tried to differentiate reality from dreams and truth from imagination. Though this made no sense, it felt too real to be a dream.

Not a dream, a nightmare.

No, not a nightmare, worse.

I pushed on, searching through the thickening fog. Condensation hung in the humid air, frizzing my red hair, yet not wet enough to soothe my parched lips. The mist created an impenetrable veil, separating me from where I longed to be, where I belonged. The muck below my feet transformed.

Thinner, less viscous.

It was water.

I tried to cup some in the palm of my hand, to satisfy the unquenchable thirst.

I couldn't. It was rising, too much and too fast.

I gasped for air as I sank deeper, fluid filling my lungs.

Unlike the stagnant muck of before, this water was rapid in its movement.

A waterspout.

Swirling.

A current—a riptide.

I had visions of water circling in a bathtub, being sucked down the drain.

My body flailed at its disposal.

Around and around I went.

I pushed upward with all my might, trying to fight the current. My arms swam outward, my legs kicked.

Again, the water grew thicker, too thick to navigate.

A light appeared, distant, much like a lighthouse barely visible upon a fog-filled jetty. I reached toward the glow, but it was too far away. An optical illusion or perhaps heaven's welcome.

The more I fought, the weaker I became.

"Reid," I called out, yet my voice didn't register. One can't speak aloud when drowning.

Was I dying?

Was this what it was like?

"I'm sorry. I'm sorry I can't fight harder." The words weren't audible, yet I heard them, felt them resonate in my heart and soul.

Had I told my husband I loved him?

I said it daily, multiple times a day.

Would he know that he was in my thoughts as I stopped fighting?

I exhaled one last time, giving way to sheer exhaustion.

My eyes opened to darkness.

Had time passed?

I couldn't be sure, but no longer were my lungs unable to expand. I could breathe.

Large gulps of air. The rush gave fuel to the simmering fire from before, bringing back the torment as the flames raging through me. As the blaze flourished, my skin chilled, cooled by...

More water?

"Float, Lorna," I told myself.

I'd read that somewhere.

Don't fight—float.

The surreal sensation was of buoyancy. My body bobbed like a buoy in the waves. It was as if I were transported back to the Dead Sea. Everyone and everything floated in the Dead Sea as salt pellets the size of snowballs formed on the sand below the water.

Exhaustion dampened the flames, filling my arms and legs with heaviness.

Sleep. I needed sleep.

Drifting.

Nothingness prevailed.

Time was irrelevant.

I woke with a start—a crash—as my body landed upon a hard surface, my head bouncing as the throbbing resumed and a gush of air expelled from my lungs. Yet I was no longer in the sea, tide, or muck. The world was still dimmed but not as dark as before.

It was as if I was at the point where light and dark meet.

Dusk or dawn, which would win?

Below me was a solid surface surrounded by nothingness. I strained to hear—anything—nothing.

I spat the copper taste of blood from my dry, bloated lips as strands of my hair stuck to my battered cheeks. My swollen eyelids fluttered against a rough fabric. My shoulders ached.

I tried to move. Each attempt met unrelenting resistance.

My wrists were bound behind my back. My ankles bound to one another.

My knees bent as I inched upon the hard, cold surface with only the sounds of my own breath gasping for air and the thump of my pulse echoing in my ears. I pushed with my toes, realizing that my shoes were gone. Arching my back caused pain to radiate from my ribs. With Herculean effort, I rolled to my back, breathing in and out. When the pain subsided, I tried again, moving my legs as my fingers clawed at the smooth, cool, damp floor.

What was my last recollection—before the fire and muck?

Where had I been?

Where am I now?

Each question filled my mind with terror.

"Reid."

I didn't utter his name aloud.

This wasn't a nightmare.

This was worse.

If this was the dusk as darkness fell, would I see the dawn?

Tears prickled my eyes as I become conscious of my situation. It was what my husband and others had cautioned me about since the day I agreed to be his wife.

The wife of one of the top officers in the Sparrow army would never be fully safe.

Reid vowed to do everything he could. He wasn't alone. All of the men—Mason, Sparrow, and Patrick—my friends and family, vowed to protect me, to lay down their lives for the Sparrow world, for Sterling Sparrow, and for each of the women—Araneae, Laurel, Madeline, and me—the women they loved.

Slowly, I made my way along the cold concrete until I reached what I presumed was a wall. I whimpered as shearing pain radiated from my torso, and I moved to sit. The tears came without thought, soaking the blindfold and tracking down my cheeks until they dripped from my jaw. The salty liquid and running nose burned my dry, cracked lips. By the time I was sitting, with my hands secured behind me, I laid my head against the rough wall and sighed.

If I was here—wherever here was—what did that mean about my husband, family, and friends?

Had they laid down their lives?

Was I the last one left?

I silently prayed that everyone else was safe, that this was only me. If that were the case, I had confidence in the Sparrow men. They wouldn't stop until I was found, until whoever dropped me upon the hard floor paid.

If I was right, I would see the dawn, but my captor wouldn't.

"Oh God. Reid," I whispered, this time aloud, to the damp darkness and solitude.

The sound of movement came from my side.

I wrenched back, unable to judge distance.

Would I encounter rats or large insects?

Unwanted images with fangs and claws filled my thoughts.

"Lor-na? I-is that you?"

My neck snapped upward as I turned my face to the familiar voice.

Oh dear God, no.

"Lor-na?" My name came between sobs. "I-I thought I was alone."

My kidnapping would result in death. Of that I was certain. The abduction of the king's wife, the queen of the Sparrow outfit, would result in all-out war.

Would Chicago survive?

"Lor-na?"

"Araneae?" I asked the darkness.

REID

"*W*hat else do we know?" Patrick asked aloud to the screen protruding from the large table within Sparrow's bird plane.

At the moment, as the four of us—Sparrow, Mason, Patrick, and I—flew thousands of feet above the ground, my colleague and friend Patrick Kelly was the only voice of reason. I sure as fuck wasn't. My wife, Mason's sister, was unreachable, as was Araneae, Sterling Sparrow's wife.

"Sir," Garrett said through the screen, "Mrs. Kelly and Mrs. Pierce are safe. They're groggy, but the doctor has confirmed they're all right."

Groggy meant one thing—somehow, they'd been tranquilized.

Patrick stood taller.

"And Mrs. Kelly's baby wasn't affected."

We all looked his direction. It must be a difficult place for him to be, to be happy when two of our wives were missing. "Where are Mrs. Pierce and Mrs. Kelly?" Mason asked.

"They're secured within the main house office." As one of our most trusted capos, Garrett had been the one charged with protecting all of our wives. The reason the ladies were in Montana was a long story. What mattered right now was why no one could reach Lorna or Araneae.

I looked over at Sterling Sparrow, the kingpin of Chicago's underground. His suit coat and tie were missing. The sleeves on his starched white shirt were rolled to his elbows, and his dark eyes simmering with rage met mine. The stress he was unsuccessfully hiding showed in the strain of his muscles—tendons pulled tight in his neck, his jaw rigid, and a vein bulging on his forehead.

"Where the fuck were you?" Sparrow bellowed.

The leader of the Sparrow outfit has run the gamut of emotions in the last few hours, as I have. Currently, our plan was to stay on topic and save our rage for those who deserved it.

"Mr. Sparrow, I was at Seth's. As I said, he'd reported a problem with the security. We thought it was a power issue. There had been a lightning storm the night before. We thought maybe a breaker was blown or a line down. He'd sent out some hands to check the wires. The women were in the main house. When I left them, the house was still online." He paused. "And I'd left Antonio to watch the immediate grounds."

I shook my head. Seth was a ranch hand turned ranch manager who cared for Mason's land and livestock as if they were his own. Antonio was a Sparrow. Yes, *was*. Upon Garrett's return to the main house, Antonio was discovered in one of the outbuildings with a bullet through the back of his head.

Laurel, Mason's wife, was a bio-researcher. Madeline, Patrick's wife, was thirty-three weeks pregnant. Prior to the house going off-line, Laurel had been in the secure office and Madeline had been upstairs napping. They were present and accounted for. The two ladies who were now unreachable—I refused to use the term missing—Araneae and Lorna, were in the kitchen.

"You've searched the house and grounds?" I asked again.

"Yes, sir." He stared into the camera. "It seems like it was a fast snatch. Mrs. Sparrow and Mrs. Murray were the most easily accessible. The kidnappers didn't search for the other two women."

My teeth ached as I clenched tighter.

"I've double- and triple-checked," Garrett continued. "No one came on the property via automobile. All the access roads are locked and gated."

"How about by horse?" Mason asked. "They could come from any direction on horseback."

Horseback was a common mode of transportation as well as off-road vehicles. Mason's property covered over ten thousand acres, complete with mountains and valleys. It was quite the increase from his original property. If he had his way, he'd acquire more to keep it from being turned into anything other than its natural beauty.

"There are hoofprints," Garrett said, "but sir, you have a corral. We can't differentiate your horses' prints from someone else's."

Sparrow turned to me. "Trackers? Why aren't they broadcasting?"

The signals we could isolate were either coming from the tower in Chicago or the main house at the ranch. "Garrett," I said, "Mrs. Murray's and Mrs. Sparrow's purses and shoes. Did they take them with them?"

"I haven't inspected their private rooms other than to know they aren't there. I don't know what was taken with them."

"They were wearing shoes at least," Sparrow said, referring to the trackers all of the ladies knew were contained in their shoes and purses. It wasn't an overt mode of control. It was what we all said, for their safety. "They should be able to be isolated."

I shook my head. "If they were wearing them, the only way to stop the transmission would be to destroy their shoes or block the transmission."

"That's not easy to do," Mason added. "Only a container lined in a special polymer could do that." Mason stood and ran his fingers through his long hair. His colorful bicep bulged beneath his sleeve as my brother-in-law worked to contain his anger. He faced me. "I know we're all stressed out, but I need to access my security system. It's fucking insane that there are parts still off-line."

I turned to the screen. "The ladies are groggy. What does the doctor think caused it?"

"She couldn't say. She did take blood and saliva samples to do a toxicology screen."

"Go through all the food and drink, find out what they consumed," Sparrow said.

"Mrs. Pierce has already begun," Garrett said. "If it's all right with you, for now I would feel better staying close to Mrs. Kelly and Mrs. Pierce. No one will get near them."

We all nodded.

"Please let us know when you land," Garrett said. "I know the ladies are anxious for your arrival."

"Yes," Patrick replied. "Stay in the home office. It's secure."

The office in the original home was secure too, but that's another long story.

The screen went black as Garrett disconnected.

The entire room exhaled.

The four of us had been together for nearly two decades, meeting on our way to basic training. In a nutshell, that time spent together in training and our tours of duty solidified our bond. Once we had satisfied our military obligations, we all came back to the States, and with the help of the GI bill and Sterling Sparrow, we went to college, completing our degrees while pursuing and perfecting our knowledge and skills in preparation for the next step.

We spearheaded the coup to take over the Sparrow outfit.

Sterling Sparrow's father, Allister Sparrow, had been in charge for too long. When it came to his son, Allister wore blinders, underestimating both Sterling and his chosen ring of advisors—us.

On a cold winter's night, Allister Sparrow met his demise, falling from a construction-site beam, a tragic accident. Or so it appeared. As luck, providence, or maybe karma would have it, his fall came after Sterling Sparrow secured his father's golden ring, the one with the family crest, as well as his father's empire.

From that day forward, Sterling Sparrow reigned in his rightful position as the kingpin of Chicago. At the time, the dynasty was shared with another outfit. It was an agreement Allister had made when the four of us were children.

Over three years ago, the other kingpin was exposed for his role in human trafficking, and Sparrow became the sole ruler of the third-largest city in the United States.

Every day since has been a challenge to maintain that status.

There was no doubt that whatever was occurring with Lorna and Araneae was related to Sterling Sparrow's reign. No one would take the queen of Chicago without expecting a fight. If that was what they wanted, we were on our way to give it.

Mason's ongoing words pulled me from my thoughts. "...need access. Once I have it..."

Technology was my thing. Artificial intelligence was his.

Money trails were Patrick's. As a team we were nearly unstoppable. However, at the moment, I wasn't thinking straight. My mind wasn't on the possible culprit or how to find them through technology and possibly the dark web. My thoughts were zeroed in on one woman. When I closed my eyes, I saw her vibrant green stare, tasted her luscious lips, and felt the warmth of her soft skin under my touch.

I remembered every word from our telephone conversation earlier this morning. I recalled the last time we were together, when we kissed goodbye before I returned to Chicago, leaving her on Mason's ranch. I recollected our first kiss and the last time we'd made love. Every minute we'd shared was right there in my thoughts, every fucking scene, the way Lorna looked, smelled, felt, and tasted, the sound of her voice, her laughter, and her noises she made during pleasure.

"Reid," Mason said, reaching for my arm, pulling me from my thoughts.

I yanked my arm away as I set my jaw. "What?" My gaze darkened. "You said your ranch was safe." I stood. "My wife is missing." I'd said the word—missing.

I fucking hated it, but I said it.

"Man, she's my fucking sister. Do you think I would have purposely put her or" —he looked to Sparrow— "Araneae in danger? Lorna's my sister," he repeated.

Standing to my full height, my chest met his. "She's my *wife*."

"She was my sister first."

Patrick stepped closer, moving his gaze from me to Mason and back before he nodded. "Now that we have all the family relationships settled, we need to concentrate on finding them."

Neither Mason nor I blinked, both still staring at one another.

It was Patrick who spoke again. "Lorna is someone special to all of us. She's my friend and Sparrow's. Hell, she put up with us when…"

"When she wasn't wanted?" I said, finishing his sentence.

"No," Patrick said.

I turned to Sparrow, my dark eyes narrowing. "You didn't want her in the tower. You tried to send her away, some other place where you didn't have to see her every day." I didn't add the most important part, the part where Lorna reminded him of Mason and how Sparrow had screwed up. That reason no longer applied, but the memories were there and fuck if I could forget them.

Forgive and forget.

Hell, it wasn't as easy as it sounded.

Sparrow turned to face us. "You're right. I wanted Lorna someplace else, someplace *safe*" —his volume rose— "nine fucking years ago." He stepped closer. "In case you've forgotten, my wife is also missing—my pregnant wife. I'd sell what's left of my fucking soul if I could have them all right now in a villa in the South of France or on an isle in Greece. So instead of bitching, maybe you can admit I was right."

Mason, Sparrow, and I exchanged looks. There was so

much that could be conveyed with just our eyes. While Mason had been the one to bring Lorna to our tower, he wasn't the one who convinced her to stay. That was me.

I was the one who put and kept her in danger with that first kiss.

I lifted my hand. "You were right." I took a step back and collapsed into one of the four secured chairs ringing the round table.

Farther back in the aft of the plane was a large media area, bedroom, multiple bathrooms, a kitchen area and a lounge the crew used. Yes, this was an airplane, but it wasn't your standard Cessna. This one was customized, all the way to the bird-like paint job on the exterior. We weren't arriving to Montana undercover. We were making a statement, as were the two other planes of capos. No fucking stone would be left unturned.

I peered up at my friends. "This is my fault."

"How the fuck are you to blame?" Sparrow asked.

REID

Sparrow's question rang in my ears as the plane continued flying west. "How the fuck are you to blame?"

"I was the one who wanted Lorna to stay. If I would have walked away from her and let you have your way, she would be safe and happy in a quaint English village."

"If that's the case," Sparrow said, sitting beside me, his dark brown orbs looking directly into mine, "Araneae is my fault. If I could have walked away from what my father promised and allowed Kennedy Hawkins to continue her career in fashion, she could have met a nice, safe man, and right now be living a regular life in a small house in Denver, with a dog and 2.5 kids."

"I brought Lorna to the tower," Mason said, also sitting.

"She's my sister. If anyone is responsible for her, it's me. It always has been."

"Fuck this, you assholes," Patrick said.

We all turned his direction.

"Yes, Mason," Patrick began as he paced back and forth, "you brought Lorna to the tower—why? Because you thought it was best." Patrick turned to me. "And you, hell, Reid, you fell in love with her. How fucking terrible for you both. I'm sure isolation in a country where she had to drive backward would have been a better route." His blue gaze went to Sparrow. "And I'm damn sure Araneae hasn't lamented the loss of safe and boring. That woman is many things; none of them is boring. You two fucking belong together." His Adam's apple bobbed as he took us all in. "Get your goddamned heads in the game. It wasn't that long ago you basically told me the same thing. I don't have to guess what it feels like to have the woman who you love missing. I know. I knew for longer than" —he looked at his watch— "six or seven hours. I pray to God —if he exists—that you never have to live with that feeling for as many years as I did."

The room fell silent. Only the roar of the plane's engines humming in the background registered as Patrick's words settled around us.

He was right—the voice of reason.

Infighting wouldn't benefit Lorna or Araneae.

Mason spoke. As he did, his cadence was calmer than before, his words more pronounced, thought-out, and distinct. "I know it's not Laurel who is missing, and I'm thankful for that." He turned to Patrick. "Or Madeline." He looked at Sparrow and me. "They're your wives, not mine or Patrick's, but as I've mentioned, Lorna's my sister, and I'm not losing another one of those." He looked directly at Sparrow. "Or my best friend's wife. Fuck, Patrick's right. I wasn't here when you two found one another, but I'd bet she gave you hell."

Despite the circumstances, we all briefly grinned.

"I am certain," Mason continued, "there's no other woman in the world who would put up with your sorry ass." He smirked. "She gives you as much shit as you shovel out, which is glorious to watch. You two were meant for one another. And that kid she's carrying, he or she has an empire to inherit. We're getting them all back."

Patrick exhaled and took the final seat at the table. He placed his hands palms down on the surface and leaned forward. "Are we good?"

We all looked around, to our friends, our colleagues, and the men we all trusted more than any other souls on this earth. We hadn't let the US Army, a war, organizing a coup, or even the death of a close friend separate us.

"I'm good," I said. "I guess I want to kick your asses because you're here" —I grinned— "and because I can."

Scoffs and murmurs of disagreement abounded.

"Whoever did this is dead," I said, the humor suddenly absent from my voice.

Everyone nodded.

"I'm good."

"Good."

"I'm good."

Patrick nodded. "All right, we move on. Whether Lorna and Araneae are the loves of our lives or simply women we love—because whether there is blood or not, we're a fucking family—we all have a stake in their safe recovery. Agreed?"

"Agreed," came from all around the table.

"After we sit down with Garrett," Patrick said, back on business, "and learn all he knows, we're sending him back to Chicago."

"Why?" I asked.

"We need him there," Patrick said. "If this is a diversion" —he looked around the table— "it's fucking working. Look what it's doing to us. Imagine the rumors flying through the ranks. We can't leave Chicago without a leader. Garrett is the closet capo we have to a number three, or in our case number five. That's why we trusted him with the women. With all four of us in Montana, Chicago is vulnerable. And that might have been the fucking plan.

"We need him there. The Sparrow capos know and respect Garrett. We can't have anyone further down the line fill that position." Patrick sat taller, pulling his hands from the table. "Plus, I trust him."

"He fucked up," Mason replied.

Patrick shook his head. "Whatever the fuck happened would have happened whoever was on the ranch." He turned to Mason. "We need to figure out who is capable of hijacking your security. Someone knows their shit. This wasn't a chance kidnapping. This was planned and well executed. Garrett was probably right. The two most accessible women were taken. We need to figure out by whom.

"First, we are getting Lorna and Araneae back. Despite the way it looks, I believe Garrett and Antonio are the reason all four women aren't missing. Their presence made the kidnappers act quickly."

Mason nodded. "I've been thinking about the security system we put into place when we rebuilt the house on my ranch. I was fucking sure it was hack-proof. But right now, with the data we retrieved, we're missing nearly thirty minutes. It's a black hole. There's no fucking way to hijack the entire system, not unless you know exactly what we did to create it."

I thought about that too. What we'd done was unique. We'd created the system as a hybrid of multiple top-notch systems. I nodded as I hit a button to lift the screen before me. Even though we were on our way from Chicago to Montana, I could access our main system back in Chicago, the one in our tower. It wouldn't be as fast. That was why I usually stayed behind. I worked the keyboards while Sparrow, Patrick, and Mason hit the ground running.

This time was different.

This was my wife.

There weren't enough chains to keep me in Chicago. I had to be wherever my wife was. I began to type upon the keyboard, accessing our mainframe.

"Seven hours since the system went black," Sparrow said,

standing with his grip on the back of the chair, his knuckles blanching from the pressure. "Six fucking hours since we got the first call." He looked at Patrick. "I need a list of everyone and anyone that knows that fucking ranch exists and belongs to Mason."

Patrick nodded as he too began typing away at another keyboard.

We were flying above the clouds.

Beyond the small rectangular windows, the sun shone brightly, reflecting off the billows of white. On the ground, it could be gray and cloudy, yet we couldn't see it. That was how this scenario felt. The answer could be as close as the underside of the clouds, yet we couldn't see it.

The plane continued west, toward the sun.

The first call had come to us at 2:20 p.m. Chicago time, an hour ahead of Mason's ranch. The first message was that Antonio wasn't responding. I immediately tried to access the ranch. When I couldn't, I called Mason. He was away from the tower, as were Sparrow and Patrick, all three in three different locations.

They'd all had fires to extinguish.

Day in and day out, there has been so much shit happening lately. Little fires—some literally—everywhere. Explosions. Missing merchandise. Raids. Warrants. Fighting among the ranks. Gang against gang disputes. The list went on and on.

It wasn't only the Sparrow outfit that had been inundated.

Our allies—the Detroit bratva, a smaller organization in

the region, our cohort in Denver, and even those in New Orleans—were also fighting a barrage of stupid incidents. For the last two months, it had been as if we and our allies were being systematically tested.

One incident was a series of small car explosions in the public parking garage of our tower. That was too close to home for any of us. It was then that Sparrow decided our wives needed to be away from the tower, away from Chicago. We analyzed each of our retreats. I used the term *our*, yet I didn't own a retreat, not like the other three men.

Patrick's, on Padre Island, Texas, officially belonged to his daughter. Sparrow's, in Ontario, belonged to him through an LLC. Travel to his cabin required crossing the border, something that of late was getting more complicated. Mason's in nowhere Montana made the most sense.

He'd purchased the ranch through a shell company a few years ago, from himself. Of course, when he'd owned it at first, it had not been under his legal name. The trail of transactions was long and difficult to navigate. Taking our wives to the ranch seemed to be the best answer.

Lockdown could be arduous within three stories of a glass tower. All of the women had expressed their dissension on multiple occasions. The four of us agreed that having fresh air, mountains, and thousands of acres would help the women feel less cooped up.

I stopped typing upon the keyboard and looked up.

Patrick and Mason were working on the keyboards before them. Sparrow was standing, his hand on the wall above a window as he stared out the small pane of glass. His expression was a combination of rage and sadness, determination and helplessness. His wife, the woman he vowed to love and protect, was in danger. I knew what he was thinking because I was thinking the same thing.

"This, whatever this is, has been in the works for a while," I said.

Sparrow turned my way. "I was thinking the same thing."

"We figure out who has been testing us, pushing us and our allies recently, and we know who to blame."

"Right now, I want the women back," Sparrow said. "After that, we can fucking scorch the entire country, the world, I don't give a shit."

Patrick looked up from the keyboard. "They know that."

"Know what?" I asked.

"Anyone who dared to take our women knew what the end result would be."

"You think," Sparrow asked, walking toward the table, "that is what they want?"

I shrugged. "It's not out of the realm of possibility. The guilty party wants destruction and what better way to get it than to let the Sparrows do it?"

"I'm in the system at the ranch," Mason said. He looked up, his green eyes gleaming. "We put in this backdoor access." His head shook. "Holy shit."

LORNA

"**Y**es, it's me," Araneae said as she scooted closer. "Are you...hurt? Did they hurt you?"

Was I hurt?

"I'm, I-I don't know. I feel so odd." Of course I felt odd. I was bound in a dark, cold place, but it was more. "Jittery and disoriented. Like I don't know how much time has passed." Her shoulder brushed mine. I leaned closer. "My hands are—"

"Mine too," she said, her voice stronger than before.

"What about you? Did they hurt you?"

"I think I stopped them. There must have been something in the lemonade we were drinking."

Lemonade?

I tried to think back. "I-I'm having trouble remembering," I confessed.

"Don't you remember? We were in Laurel and Mason's

kitchen at the ranch. We'd finished lunch. Maddie went upstairs, and Laurel went to the office."

As Araneae spoke, the scene came back to me. I recalled the serenity of the kitchen with the spectacular view from the attached patio and the seclusion of the ranch in the midst of the surreal beauty of the Montana landscape. For a woman who'd lived her entire life in the concrete jungle of Chicago, I found everything about the ranch stunning.

I recalled eating lunch, the four of us. We'd all put our own plates together and poured our own drinks. I couldn't come up with how our lemonade had been drugged. No one else had been within the house.

"Are they...? Maddie and Laurel...are they here?"

"No one else is," Araneae replied. "Well, until now. You are."

She was now close enough that I could feel the warmth of her skin, her arm next to mine moving as she spoke. It wasn't much of a connection while at the same time it was monumental. For a moment, I savored the bond. Any warmth was better than the cold floor and rough wall.

"I'm sorry you're here and we're alone," I said. "How is the baby?"

"I wish I was alone." She quickly added, "Because I don't want anyone else to suffer. The baby..." Her arm moved up and then down as if she'd shrugged. "I think the baby is all right. I told them. As soon as I woke, I told them I was pregnant and if they didn't hurt me or my baby, my husband would pay anything." She took a ragged breath. "I think it worked. I couldn't see, but I think from what I heard, one man convinced the other not to inject me with something."

There was no doubt that her husband would pay. He'd also make whoever this was pay. The truth was that without Sterling Sparrow, Araneae Sparrow was more than capable of bankrolling her own ransom. It was a complicated story, but the end of it was that she inherited a large sum of money in stocks. Together with her husband, they were extremely wealthy.

While Sparrow's dealing may not always be legal, Araneae decided to use her wealth in a more philanthropic way, creating the Sparrow Institute, a foundation that aided and benefitted victims of human trafficking.

I thought about what she said, about stopping an injection. "Maybe that's what happened to me. I was hallucinating." My pulse thumped faster. "Do you think they gave me something? A drug?"

"I don't know," Araneae admitted. "Are you feeling any better?"

"My head still hurts. Earlier, I felt like I was struggling to walk, and then there was water." I shook my head. "But I'm dry, not wet. I don't know what was real." I took a deep breath and winced. "My ribs are sore." I moved my tongue around my mouth. "And I'm thirsty. My mouth feels like a desert."

"I'm sorry," she said.

"Why are you sorry?"

"Maybe they hurt you because they don't want to hurt me."

I laid my head on her shoulder. Araneae was easily five inches taller than me. If I could have reached for her hand, I would have. In this instant, I recalled the first time I met her, when she first was brought to our tower.

The second our gazes met and her lips curled into a smile, the trepidation I'd anticipated at the addition of another woman to our family disappeared. Araneae was the only woman in the world who could simultaneously put up with and love Sterling Sparrow. I have no idea how a decades-old prophecy could be so incredibly spot-on, but it was.

And through the years to follow, Araneae became more than Sparrow's future; she eased her way into all of our lives. A friend. A confidant. A sister. A queen. She took her rightful place beside the most powerful man in the city, one of the most powerful men in the country, and has made a name for herself as a kind, generous, loving, and compassionate soul, a lady who would do anything in the world for those she loved and those in need, while staying strong enough to do whatever was necessary. If the situation required a fight, she was a tiger. If a verbal duel was asked, she was locked and loaded with the mouth of a sailor. If the circumstances required finesse to manipulate that powerful man behind the scenes, she was beyond capable.

From that first moment I saw her in the penthouse kitchen, I knew she was meant to be a part of us—our family. Laying my head upon her shoulder was the only way, at this moment, I could connect to her. "We're getting out of here together."

Her head came in contact with mine. "Damn right."

We both grew deadly silent at the clicking sound of a locking mechanism and then a door moving across the concrete floor. My pulse sped up as beyond the blindfold, there was suddenly light. I lifted my face, wondering if I could see.

All I could make out were boots and jeans. There were two sets, two men.

"Looks like they finally woke," a man's deep voice said.

My arm trembled against Araneae's as I willed myself to have strength to face whatever was to come. The two sets of feet paced before us, their boots clicking on the hard floor.

"Which one of you is married to Price?"

Price?

"Mrs. Price?" another man asked.

"Price?" we both questioned.

A boot nudged at my leg. "Answer the fucking question."

My head shook from side to side. "Neither of us." I wasn't certain how much information to share.

"You," the man said. But no longer was I being nudged.

"Don't fucking touch me," Araneae said. "I don't know anyone named Price."

"It was his house where they found you."

They?

Did that mean that these people weren't the ones who took us?

"Pierce," a woman's voice said. I lifted my chin to see her

shoes and legs as she entered the room. "His name is Pierce," she said. "Edgar Price was an alias." This woman was our third visitor, not one of the men who'd first walked in. Her steps were lighter and her shoes daintier. Heels. I saw the pointed toes peering beneath flowing black slacks as she stepped. "They failed. She isn't one of them." It was a final statement, not looking for debate. "The imbeciles brought us the wrong women. Two opportunities and they failed. If they do it again, they won't live to have another opportunity."

The woman came closer and lifted my chin. I wanted to back away, but there was nowhere for me to go. Her grasp turned my head from side to side. "She needs ice for her cheek." The woman then stepped over to Araneae. "And this one says she's pregnant?"

"I am," Araneae said. "Five and a half months."

"Neither one of you is Pierce's wife, the scientist?" a man asked.

"No," Araneae answered. "We're not. You don't want to know who my husband is."

"Honey," the woman replied, "I don't give a fuck who he is or who you are for that matter. Currently, you're nothing more than an irrelevant inconvenience."

"He'll pay," Araneae replied. "My husband will. Name a price."

"We're not after money." Her shoes clipped over the concrete. "But...this has possibilities."

The woman's steps moved farther away. With the light on, I took inventory of what I could see by raising my chin. It wasn't much, but the small gap near my nose allowed me to see the two men's boots, the legs of their jeans, and the woman's shoes and slacks. I could also see that across the room, roughly twelve feet away, was a toilet and sink. If I turned my head a bit, there appeared to be a bunk bed—I could only see the bottom bunk, but the structure suggested an upper bunk too—similar to what I'd seen in movies of prisons or jail cells.

We were in a prison cell.

"They're fucking morons," the woman declared.

Who did she mean?

"You kidnapped us. Who's the moron?" Araneae asked.

The woman quickly stepped back to Araneae. "Listen, bitch. Right now, your days are at my disposal. If you're really pregnant, I suggest you keep your damn mouth closed."

"She is," I volunteered.

"Get her ice and" —she stood between our two sets of bound legs— "if you two can behave, this might work out. When Jet comes back, he'll have ice and bottles of water. Keep your mouths shut and don't fight. It's either your lucky day or your luck has run out. Neither of you is who we want. When he returns, Jet will cut the tape on your arms and legs. Once he's out of the room and the door is locked, you can take off the blindfolds. Do it sooner and the privilege is gone." She again reached for my chin and lifted it higher. "Do we have a deal?"

"Yes," I answered, fearful Araneae may fight.

She was a tiger and now a caged one. However, in our

current position, fighting wouldn't do either of us any good. I loved my friend, but the difficulties she'd experienced in her life were tame compared to where Mason and I had grown up.

I wasn't a pushover, but I also wasn't stupid. The best thing for us to do was cooperate, figure this shit out, and get free.

"You?" the woman questioned. "Deal?"

I nudged Araneae's arm.

"Yes," she mumbled through clenched teeth.

From the slit below my blindfold, I watched as all three sets of feet moved to the far side and disappeared behind the closing door. To my joy, the light was still on. I whispered, "Can you see at all?"

"I want them all dead."

I nodded. "I agree, but we have to cooperate."

"I want Sterling to—"

"Araneae," I interrupted, "what did you get out of that question-and-answer session?"

Her voice changed. "You need ice. Lorna, why do you need ice?"

"My face...my cheeks feel swollen and sore."

"Fucking—"

"No," I said. "Price, Edgar Price, and then they said Pierce. That woman said we weren't who she wanted. She wants—"

"Laurel," we both said together.

REID

The plane touched down at the closest excuse for an airport near Mason's ranch. Truth be told, it wasn't much of an airport. While the two runways were recently paved with expensive-looking lights, the only building nearby couldn't even pass as a hangar. Marianne would need to fly to Bozeman or Butte for fuel before flying Garrett back to Chicago. I supposed we could have flown to one of those cities and traveled here, perhaps via helicopter. That would have required more time, time none of us were willing to sacrifice.

As I descended the steps, I found myself too consumed to notice the beauty that this landscape usually provided. The mountains held my interest for less than a second. The dried grass, brush, and fences were lost to thoughts of my wife.

Even in the summertime, the mountain peaks in the

distance were capped in white snow. It was as if the writer of the song "America the Beautiful" had pictured these mountains when she created the lyric, "purple mountain majesties." For a moment, I recalled how much Lorna had loved the views when we were here for Mason and Laurel's wedding and then again, a couple of weeks ago before we'd separated.

During that stay, Lorna and I rode a couple of Mason's horses, just the two of us, into a valley, a bowl he called it. We'd packed a picnic and stopped near a river. It was nothing like I'd known growing up in a Chicago suburb. There were no paved streets. No brick apartment buildings. No row of houses. There was only nature.

"Reid," Sparrow said.

"Yes?" I replied, shaking off the memory the view evoked.

"We need you. Keep your head in the game."

I couldn't let myself slip into the black hole of memories of my wife. There were too many. I could be lost for days.

"I'm here," I said as I followed the other three men into a waiting large SUV. The man driving was a trusted employee of Mason's ranch. Patrick took the front passenger seat, Sparrow and I sat in the middle, and Mason did his best to fit into the third seat. His long legs came out between Sparrow's and my bucket seats.

"I could have called for two cars," Mason said, "but I thought we might want to keep brainstorming."

"Explain what you found with the security in more detail," Sparrow said to Mason.

What he meant was explain it in a way he could understand. The technical jargon was not Sparrow's specialty. It wasn't that he lacked intelligence. It was that between the four of us, we had a broad range of knowledge. I paled in comparison to Sparrow when it came to real estate and acquiring assets through legal dealings such as he did day in and day out with Sparrow Enterprises. His knowledge was hard learned from his father as well as self-taught and fueled by his education.

I was the same but with differing knowledge. I'd studied computer engineering at MIT, yet my education never stopped. Before MIT, the army was my teacher. Since, it had been life and opportunity. Patrick's education at University of Chicago Booth, Sparrow's at University of Michigan, and Mason's at Northwestern, as well as mine, were all for one reason: to make the Sparrow outfit superior, not only physically but intellectually.

"I can't get to a total of the missing thirty minutes," Mason said. "Right now, all I can confirm is that the airspace over the ranch was compromised. I'm suspecting that the kidnappers came in and went out via helicopter."

"And neither Madeline nor Laurel heard it?" I asked.

"They both fell asleep. Madeline didn't realize it was drug induced," Patrick said. "She simply thought she was tired after lunch. The baby has been zapping her energy."

"And Laurel didn't realize she'd fallen asleep until Garrett woke her," Mason added. He leaned forward between the seats. "I think we can assume the same for Lorna and Araneae. They fell asleep or were at least unaware."

"Like GHB?" Sparrow asked.

Patrick nodded. "Until we get blood tests back on Maddie and Laurel, we won't know for sure. But I've done some research. There isn't a lot known regarding GHB in pregnancy. It's believed to cross the placenta. The positive part is that the effects hit hard and the drug is quickly metabolized."

"What did the doctor who came to the ranch say?" Sparrow asked.

Patrick responded, "Laurel, Maddie, and the baby are fine. We can only assume your baby is the same."

Sparrow turned to the window as the Montana scenery passed by. "I've never felt so fucking impotent." Just as quickly, he turned back. "Who gave it to them?"

We all stared his direction.

"Think about it. The women were all drugged. The airspace was breached. Neither Laurel nor Madeline heard anything. They had to have ingested the drug prior to the kidnappers arriving. If Madeline and Laurel ingested it before they left the kitchen, when did they ingest it? Who drugged them? It couldn't be the kidnapper if he or she arrived via helicopter later."

"You're right," I said. "Seth?"

Before anyone could answer that question, Patrick turned back to us. "Garrett?"

"You said you trusted him," Mason said from the back of

the SUV.

"Who else was there?" I asked, not wanting to believe the worst about either man.

"Find out who has been in the main house in the last twenty-four hours," Sparrow said. "Every single person will come face-to-face with me. I want them at the house."

Both Patrick and Mason began typing on their phones, sending text messages to whoever could accomplish Sparrow's order.

"Garrett texted," Patrick said. "He said Laurel thinks it could have been the lemonade. It's all she can figure out that they all four consumed."

The SUV came to a large iron gate—*Jackson Ranch* embossed over the top. The ranch was named anew after a fire consumed the original main house. The name Jackson was in honor of a deceased friend of Mason's.

The gate wasn't manned with a guard but an electronic sentry. There was a camera above the gate. A code or a card was also required for entry. Each code and card were user specific. Visual as well as digital information was recorded every time a gate opened. It was the same on the other few entrances. No one came or went from the ranch without the information being recorded.

From my limited experience on Mason's land, this was the first of many checkpoints to get near the main house. Over ten thousand acres was a good amount of land. Once the gate opened, we proceeded within. The first area of habitation was the grouping of buildings that included the house where Seth, the ranch manager, lived with his wife and two children. Over the last year, a sizeable addition had been added for his growing family, giving it a statelier appearance.

Besides the multiple barns and outbuildings, this was where the ranch hands came for their assignments. Not far up the lane was the bunkhouse. For the most part, Mason utilized seasonal workers. They were like guns for hire—cowboys who knew what to do and did it for a paycheck. It decreased personal attachment and questions that may come along due to who lived on the other side of the ravine.

The person who oversaw the ranch hands and the seasonal workers and was dedicated to the land and animals was Seth Dorgan, with help from his wife, Lindsey. Though he was young, he'd helped Mason during a difficult time, was well vetted, and exceptionally paid. In many ways, Seth treated the ranch as if it was his own. That not only suited Mason, but it meshed with the agricultural powers-that-be for the state of Montana.

Seth Dorgan was the go-to man for anything concerning the Jackson Ranch. He answered to Mason; everyone else answered to him. Mason needed that kind of loyalty with spending most of his time in Chicago.

Once the road passed the barns and outbuildings, the land cleared into fenced pastures for as far as the eye could see. Finally, we approached a large ravine with a river below. This late in the summer, the river was more of a stream. In the spring, with the snow melting from the mountains, Mason said it could overrun the banks as it raged through the gorge.

Mason's house was on the other side of the ravine. The home that had been present when he first purchased the property appealed to him in large part due to its limited accessibility.

As we canvassed the distance, it was clear that with Garrett at Seth's house, a helicopter could have come from the other direction, virtually unnoticed down at Seth's house.

The SUV continued along the packed-dirt road.

The main house was only used by Mason and Laurel as a retreat. Since they spent most of their time in Chicago, the lane we were on qualified as a road less traveled.

In the distance, the main house came into view. As it did, the energy in the SUV changed. In a few moments, Patrick and Mason would have their wives in their arms. They could look into their eyes and reassure themselves that all was right with the world.

They could.

They would.

I turned to Sparrow as he turned to me.

Wordlessly we promised one another that one day soon we too would be holding our wives.

Whoever had dared to enter this property, breach the security, and take Lorna and Araneae would pay. Of that we could be certain.

As the SUV slowed, the door upon the large porch opened.

LORNA

"*A*raneae, you have to eat," I said, looking at the food she'd been given as we sat side by side on the lower bunk, holding our plastic plates in our laps. Her disheveled long blonde hair lay over her shoulders, veiling her profile.

Pushing it aside, she turned her soft brown eyes my direction. "How do we know it's safe?"

I stared at the plate that had been given to me and taking a deep breath, lifted a forkful of what appeared to be some kind of chicken dish to my lips. After swallowing, I forced a grin. "I'd be happy to give whoever our cook is some lessons on spices. It's bland but I think edible."

Araneae pushed the chicken, rice, and sauce around the plastic plate with the plastic fork. "I want to be home." She lowered her voice. "What do you think the men...?" Her eyes glistened with unshed tears. "He's so worried. I know he is."

I nodded. "I'm sure they all are."

Leaving the food uneaten and setting the plate on the bed, Araneae stood and resumed her earlier pacing. She was still wearing the same clothes we'd dressed in this morning, soft pants and an oversized shirt. Her midsection was beginning to show a distinct roundness. She didn't have the beach ball of Madeline, but her baby bump was visible.

Araneae stopped pacing and turned to me. "Do you know what Sterling has said to me a million times?"

My lips quirked upward. "Are you sure it's something you want to share?"

A soft pink hue colored her cheeks. "I wouldn't even know where to begin with the non-sharable things he's said. What I'm thinking about is what he's said over and over again" — her voice lowered in a sad attempt to mimic Sterling's deep voice— "this is for your safety." She spun, allowing her arms and hands to tap her thighs. "Over and over to the point that when he first found me" —found was an interesting choice of word— "I hated the phrase. I hated it. Everything about it. His constant obsession with safety." She let out a long breath, lifted her chin toward the ceiling, and stared at the two bare light bulbs high above. When her gaze came back to mine, her expression was stoically strong, yet telltale tears flowed down each cheek. "But, I learned he meant well. I know he can be..."

I placed my plate beside hers on the thin mattress and stood. Walking toward her, I reached for her hands. "Overbearing, overprotective, domineering, and bossy."

With each of my adjectives, Araneae nodded and her sad smile grew. "Yes, all of those things. And I love every damn one. I wouldn't ask him to be different than he is. And he has never asked that of me. He" —she inhaled as she searched for the right words— "welcomed me as I am, never trying to change me." She swallowed. "I mean, we didn't know one another." Her head tilted. "I don't think I was what he expected."

"You weren't. You're so much more," I said.

"With him, I'm different. Sterling helped me understand who I am, who I'm capable of being. He gave me my past, my roots, and also showed me that I had wings to fly. He showed me that I could soar to untold heights. The gifts he's given me have nothing to do with possessions. He gave me security and a family." She squeezed my hand. "You, Reid, Patrick, and then everyone." She let go of my hand, peered downward, and placed hers over her baby bump. "And now our child." Looking back to me, she took a ragged breath. "I'm scared. Did we not listen to him? Did we do something wrong?"

I swallowed the emotions I didn't want to feel, ones too numerous to articulate. "No, Araneae. We were where they wanted us. We didn't do anything wrong."

"I've never" —Araneae walked a few steps, her feet bare as were mine— "had a family, not really, not since I was a teenager, not one of my own. I don't want to lose that. I don't want to lose him."

"You know they will do everything—"

"That's what I'm afraid of," she interrupted, spinning

toward me, her volume rising. "I'm scared that in their attempts to save us, something will happen to one of them." She shook her head. "I can't use those wings he's given me, not without him by my side."

I swallowed the lump forming in my throat. "I understand."

"What about Reid?"

It was my turn for tears to form. For the last few hours, I'd refused to give into them, yet they persisted, now teetering precariously upon my lids. "I love him. He's my Prince Charming." I thought about what Araneae had said. "I think I had roots when I met Reid. Mason was my family, my roots to keep me grounded and safe, but it was different with Reid. Being with him and him with me gave me substance—I hope it's the same for him. When we're together, I'm more than Lorna Pierce, more than a sister. With Reid, I've always been more. It's as if we complete one another." I scoffed. "I know that sounds cheesy."

Araneae shook her head. "No." She laughed. "Yes."

I tilted my head toward the two plates. "We need to eat. We don't know when they'll bring more or come for these."

Araneae turned a complete circle. "We're in a fucking cell."

"They'll get us out." I quickly added, "And they'll stay safe in the process."

"Are you sure?" she asked.

"Remember your first lockdown?" I asked as I sat back down and picked up her plate, handing it her direction.

Araneae reached for the plastic dish and sat beside me. "Yes, I wish we had some of that wine."

"You can't drink. Remember?"

"Circumstances being what they are, I think one glass would be acceptable." She pushed the chicken around, finally stabbing a piece. "I remember I felt very alone."

"I hate that you're here with me," I admitted, "but I'm also glad. My first lockdown and many after were spent alone."

Araneae's nose scrunched. "Didn't you say it lasted five days?"

I shook my head as the memory returned. "Not the first one. The first one was not long after Sparrow's father died...the takeover of the Sparrow outfit was happening. Mace had only recently moved me into the tower. Things were more dangerous than I realized." I smiled at the forthcoming thought. "That's why Mason kidnapped me to the tower."

"You were kidnapped?"

"No," I said with a laugh. "I teased him, telling him that was what he did. It wasn't. He was...persistent."

"A quality they all possess."

I took another bite. As I did my stomach grumbled. "I guess I am hungry. You don't have some salt or pepper on you?"

"No," Araneae answered as she lifted her feet. "I don't even have shoes." Her voice lowered again. "How do you think they knew?"

"I don't know. Reid always said that when any one of us

was away, we'd always have our phones, shoes, or purses. That's why he believed they were the best place for trackers." I turned her way. "When we're rescued, I guess we'll need to tell him he needs to up his game."

I grinned, seeing Araneae finally begin to eat. The food was bland and tasteless, but it contained nutrients that she and her baby needed.

"Your first lockdown?" she encouraged.

"Didn't end well."

"What happened?"

"Reid and I weren't married." My eyes opened wide. "We weren't even engaged. We were...secret lovers. It hadn't been going on too long. We stole moments when we could." I grinned. "It was both exciting and romantic."

"Under Mason's nose? I'm surprised you got away with it."

My mind went back to nearly a decade earlier. "Reid has always been the one to scour the web, figure out the surveillance, basically the technical one while Patrick and Mason were on the streets."

"Sterling?"

"I'm sure you know what your husband does," I replied.

"I wasn't around then. I get the feeling it was different."

I nodded. "He...carried it all." I took another bite, trying to decipher a time I hadn't considered in years. "Everything rested on him. For the coup to work, Sterling Sparrow had to show the world that he was even more capable than his father had been."

"They told you all this?"

I shook my head. "They never said a word...except once, but that was the exception. Sterling had not only the Sparrow outfit to secure and rule, but he had to maintain his public persona of Sparrow Enterprises."

"So he was fun to be around?" Araneae asked with a grin.

"Unbearable is a better word. I avoided him at all costs."

"And you and Reid...?"

"We stole moments when we could. Tension was high and there was so much happening that I think Mason was too distracted to notice what we were doing. Once I was in the tower, he could worry about other things."

"Patrick?"

I grinned. "Patrick was Patrick—the same Patrick he is today. I love my husband and brother, but Patrick is the heart of the group." My eyes opened wide. "You know, like the cricket in Pinocchio—"

"Jiminy Cricket?"

"Yeah," I replied. "The conscience, the heart, the one who notices and cares."

Araneae nodded. "I think in a way, when I first met them, I felt more comfortable with him than I did Sterling." She turned my way. "I don't mean like I was attracted."

"I know what you mean. Patrick was always the friend." I scoffed. "Of course, I never knew his secret. I just always trusted him."

"Yes."

"I'm not sure if Patrick knew before the rest of them—about me and Reid. If he did, he never said a word."

"That's Patrick," Araneae agreed.

"If I'm totally honest, I wanted Reid from the first time we met. It was...like one of those movies or books. I don't know if love at first sight exists, but curiosity, intrigue...attraction."

"I think I can concur."

"I was the one to convince Reid to keep our relationship quiet. It wasn't forever, just until things quieted down. Telling Mace would have meant telling..."

"Sterling."

"Yes. He had mentioned more than once that my presence was a distraction. That's why I started trying to help. The men would be busy day and night. I began a routine of cleaning and cooking. I started in Mace's apartment but slowly expanded to common areas. I then offered...over the years, it grew into more."

"And now there are so many of us."

"Madeline is a big help. She's really taken to wanting to know more." I thought about our friend, Patrick's wife. "We've all had such different backgrounds."

Araneae nodded as she finished the last of her meal.

"I guess," I said, "I didn't want Sparrow to think I was just taking advantage of him."

"He wouldn't..."

"Looking back, I think he was also too distracted by everything to even consider me. I was the quiet distraction until..."

"What happened?"

I took a haggard breath. "You would think this would be easier. It isn't. It's never easy to say your brother died."

"You and Reid weren't officially a couple when Mason...when the explosion...?"

I shook my head. "Not really. Literally, that same night, Mason found out about us." I rolled my eyes. "And Patrick and..."

"Sterling?"

My mind went back to that night, standing out by the apartments. The rage radiating off my brother as the wheels turned in his head, connecting the dots. The total disinterest in Sparrow's gaze as he called me a distraction, not for the first time, and the way Patrick tried to soothe the entire situation.

"Yeah," I said, taking a drink from the water bottle. "Anyway, we agreed to discuss it later. But, well...later never came, not for a long time where Mason was concerned."

"Oh goodness, Lorna. When I said I felt alone during my first lockdown, I must have sounded like a spoiled brat. Holy shit. Who told you about Mason?"

"Reid and Patrick did, together."

"What about Sterling?"

I shook my head. "He didn't speak to me or look at me. Not for a while. I know he wanted me gone, but what was he going to do, kick the sister of his dead best friend out on the street when the Sparrows were in an all-out war?"

Araneae placed her emptied plate on the floor and turned

to me. "I never...you two seem...I mean, you joke, but he loves you like he loves everyone in the tower."

I nodded. "I know. We are good." I took a deep breath. "That man of yours is complicated."

"Oh, you're telling me," she said with a smile. "I want to hear more about Reid. How did you go from secret lovers to husband and wife?"

Before I could answer, the room went dark. The chicken I'd consumed churned in my stomach as Araneae and I reached for one another's hand.

"The blindfolds," she whispered.

That was the rule the man named Jet had given us. We could remove the blindfolds as long as we put them on when someone entered the room. The turning off of the light was our warning.

"Shit." I stood, scrambling in the darkness.

"They're here," Araneae said. "I put them in my jeans' pocket."

I reached out in the darkness, feeling the piece of rough fabric. We both hurriedly secured the fabric over our eyes and resumed our seats on the bed. In the process, I stepped on the plastic plate as the plastic fork rattled against the concrete floor.

The locking mechanisms clicked and the bottom of the door moved, scuffing the cement floor as it opened inward.

REID

"They were supposed to be secured," Sparrow said, sitting forward, peering through the window of the SUV as Laurel, Madeline, and Garrett came out onto the large porch. The ladies, their hair blowing in the breeze, stepped forward toward the railing on the porch, watching as our vehicle came closer.

"I texted Garrett as soon as we entered the property," Patrick said. "He knew it would be us."

As the driver brought the SUV to a stop, the doors flew open.

While everyone got out of the SUV, consciously or unconsciously, Sparrow and I hesitated, staying back by the vehicle as Patrick and Mason hurried toward their wives. It was impossible not to appreciate their evident need to be with the one they loved. To see, touch, hold, and hear one another. They were my friends, my family, and I wanted their happiness. I was also keenly aware of the sensation of being excluded from the joy. The loss of Lorna's and Araneae's presence hung around Sparrow and I like a fog—on a clear, sunny day—a barrier keeping us from the others' happiness.

Yet before that cloud chained us in, both Madeline and Laurel came our way, Madeline first to Sparrow and Laurel to me. Their hugs wordlessly said more than I was ready to hear.

"I'm so sorry," Laurel, my sister-in-law, whispered, looking into my eyes. "I-I don't know what happened."

"We'll get them back."

The ladies changed places, Laurel going to Sparrow and Madeline to me. After her quick hug, I looked down at Madeline's even larger midsection. "How are you feeling?"

"Scared," Madeline said. "I'm scared for them."

"How are you and little Patrick?"

She smiled. "You know we haven't shared his name."

They hadn't, but they had shared his gender. Madeline and Patrick had a little boy due in six weeks.

"You both are all right?" I asked again.

She allowed a smile to come to her face. "Yes. The doctor said his heartbeat is good and he's been moving—a lot. If he stops for too long, I'm to call her."

Patrick came up beside Madeline and wrapped his arm around her waist. "I sent Sparrows to the academy. Once they have Ruby secure, we'll decide where she needs to go."

Madeline exhaled. "She just began her senior year."

Patrick shook his head. "I know and I'm sorry, but we

can't allow our daughter to be at the academy with whatever is happening."

Madeline's lips came together as her green eyes peered at her husband. I knew the look she was giving to him. It was the expression that each of the women had perfected through the years. It meant, We're talking about this more once we're alone. Since Patrick's response was a nod and a kiss to Madeline's forehead, I was certain he'd interpreted it as the same message.

As the Montana breeze blew the tall grasses and white clouds floated over Mason and Laurel's house, I looked at the grouping of those present. These were the people who meant the most to all of us. They were our loved ones; they were our weak link—our Achilles' heel. This vulnerability was why Sparrow didn't welcome Lorna with open arms all those years ago. The more of us there were, the greater our liability. And now we had two more members of our family joining us by year's end.

"Everyone inside," Sparrow said.

There was no argument as we all ascended the steps to the porch. As we waited for the women to enter first, Mason reached for my arm. "I need your help. I know you want to be out turning over every fucking rock, but your strength is behind a keyboard."

My jaw clenched.

"Listen," he went on, "I found something through that backdoor access into the security that I need to verify. I didn't mention it because" —he looked around, confirming that everyone else was now inside— "I don't fucking know what to do if it's accurate."

"What did you find?"

His head shook. "I need to do some more research. There have been other outfits having issues. Patrick can look into that. He has the contacts. Sparrow can call the other leaders." He glanced into the house. Seeing that the entry was clear, he pulled the front door closed and led me toward the porch railing. Small cyclones of dust danced on the lane, and birds flew overhead as he spoke. "I have a gut feeling that I don't like."

I stared into my brother-in-law's eyes, seeing something I also didn't like, something unusual, something akin to fear. Don't get me wrong—Mason Pierce was rarely afraid. I'd watched him in military combat as well as facing enemies on Chicago's streets. I could only recall one other time I saw the shadows now lingering in his stare. It was when he first returned to us.

"You and Sparrow," I said, "the two of you made a deal."

Mason's neck straightened and his jaw tightened as he nodded. "We did, and I believed Top."

Top was the *top* or the commander of a subversive counterterrorism government agency referred to as the Sovereign Order. Don't try to research it. You won't find a thing. The Sovereign Order doesn't officially exist, and yet Mason had been a part of it for years.

"Hell," he continued, "I had no choice but to believe him. Now I'm praying to fucking God that the gut feeling I'm having is wrong. That's where I need your help. You and I designed the security for the ranch after what happened. There's no road map, no Google search or YouTube video to give away our secrets. I need you to scour the program, find the weak link if it exists. If we can assess where and how it was breached, we'll be closer to an answer. The knowledge needed to infringe on the system we created is hardly common."

"If you're right, this—Lorna and Araneae's kidnapping— could have nothing to do with the explosions in the garage, the issues with deliveries, with any of the Sparrow or other outfits' problems."

"If I'm right," Mason said, "then we could have two separate wars happening. And again, if I'm right, the enemy we're fighting here is unlike any we've ever encountered."

The front door opened inward, stilling our conversation as Sparrow stepped out onto the porch. "Get your asses in here." He narrowed his dark gaze at both of us. "Are you going to tell me what you're discussing?"

I looked to my brother-in-law.

"Yeah," Mason said, lifting his chin. "We're going to dig deeper into the security breach, and when I have something to tell you, I will."

Sparrow walked closer to Mason, continuing until they were inches apart. "It's my wife." He pointed to me. "It's his wife. And I'm fucking responsible for their safety. Sparrow is *my* name."

Mason held his ground. "This isn't a pissing contest,

Sparrow. We don't know who took the women. We don't know what they want. So at this moment, we don't even know what their endgame is."

What Mason wasn't saying was that if he was correct and this was the Order, the kidnapping might not be about Sparrow's name or the Sparrow outfit.

"It's a war," Mason continued, "and no battle can be won without counterintelligence, without understanding the enemy. We all have our specialties; let us do ours."

Sparrow didn't respond.

Mason went on, "I'm not taking a chance on Araneae's or Lorna's life by underestimating who we're up against."

We both looked at Sparrow, awaiting his response. Underestimating was something he knew from experience not to do. He straightened his shoulders. "Dead men. That's who we're up against. That's not underestimating—that's a promise." He took a deep breath and continued, "Garrett said the other two planes of capos have landed. Unfortunately, the bunkhouse is full of ranch hands. This ranch is crawling with people preparing for the approaching winter. Every fucking one of them needs to be questioned. What did they see, hear, or anything?"

Mason nodded. "I'll get Seth to work out a schedule."

Sparrow walked to the railing. "We can't house the capos there. The bunkhouse is full with the ranch hands. Patrick is looking into finding them a place to stay that's not a million miles away."

"If Seth can get us some bunks..." Mason lifted his chin

toward the near grouping of outbuildings. "The capos can be housed out there. It's not as nice as the bunkhouse, but there's a kitchen and bathrooms. Add bunks and well, it's livable."

Sparrow sighed. "I don't want them this close to the house."

"The closest hotel is over an hour away by car."

"Talk to Seth," Sparrow said, "and we'll see what he can come up with."

My gaze caught Mason's and I nodded. "Your office?"

"Yeah," he said. "Get settled in your and Lorna's room upstairs, and I'll meet you back there."

Leaving Sparrow and Mason on the porch, I walked through the threshold of the main house thinking about the never-ending shit in our lives and probably the lives of everyone. Lorna and Araneae were missing, and we had ranch hands to question, as well as bunk beds and bedding to acquire. There would be the feat of feeding the capos while setting their assignments.

It was the mundane crap that never ended.

I stilled in the foyer and looked all around. With the early evening sun streaming through the windows, the interior was bathed in golden light, making the varying shades of wood glisten. In many ways, Mason's home reminded me of Sparrow's cabin in Canada, and yet it was different. Both places were rustic in design with an overabundance of wood, from the walls, to the beams, to the floors.

This house differed in size and decoration. It was grand in

the way a main house should be, yet it wasn't majestic like Sparrow's place in Canada. Mason's house was a home. Sparrow's was a log cabin castle to go along with his castle in the sky. While he claimed he didn't want the mansion where he grew up and his mother still lived, he'd recreated it in two other forms.

This home was grand and minimalistic at the same time, reflecting both Mason's and Laurel's personalities. It was who they were individually as well as together.

I peered toward the long staircase that led upstairs. *"Get settled in your and Lorna's room upstairs."* Mason's orders. I looked down at my empty hands. I'd thrown a few things in a suitcase before we left Chicago. At this second, I wasn't even certain where it was. There was nothing urging me upward.

Our room.

A room Lorna and I had shared.

A bed we'd shared.

An empty room.

An empty bed.

Voices came from the kitchen like a safety net pulling me away from my fear and sadness.

I could enter the kitchen and find Madeline, Laurel, and Patrick. Instead, I turned as Mason and Sparrow entered from the porch.

"Have you been upstairs?" Mason asked.

I shook my head. "When they bring in my stuff, just have them put it in the room—the one where I stayed before. I don't need to get settled. I need to find Lorna and Araneae."

Sparrow's dark gaze met mine before he walked past us to the kitchen.

"Is he okay?" I asked Mason.

"No. None of us are." He motioned toward the living room and beyond with his chin. "Come with me to the office."

LORNA

The tower - nine years ago

*L*ying back on the pillow, I looked up into Reid's eyes, staring into their depths. Emotions like cyclones swirled in the deepest brown I'd ever seen. "You're worried," I said as he teased a stray strand of my red hair away from my face.

His head shook as he feigned a smile. "You're so damn beautiful."

My fingertips roamed over his chestnut skin, feeling his bare shoulders, muscular back, and firm ass. Each indentation, each tightening muscle was a story written in Braille, a masterpiece I wanted to read over and over until I knew every chapter, line, and word by heart.

"Back at you," I purred, holding him tighter as we lay

melded together, my body still reveling in the aftershocks of our stolen moment.

Our time together wouldn't last. It never did, yet in the few weeks we'd been together, I'd become addicted to his touch and the way he could orchestrate not only my body but my mind. When we were together, I believed in the fairy tale I'd been sold as a child. In his arms, my thoughts filled with possibilities for a future I'd never before dared to consider.

Never before had there been a man who so fully consumed my being. It wasn't that Reid took, but that in giving, he created a desire within me to give in return. Never had I been loved so thoroughly, not only physically—something he did beyond my wildest imagination—but emotionally too. Without knowing all of my past, in this short time Reid had shown me what a real man could be.

Of course, I had my brother, but beyond that, my examples of men were poor at best and more often horrible. The only thing the men my mother had attracted taught me was to never trust, depend upon, or give my love to a man. And yet Reid Murray was nothing like those men of my childhood. He had not only the honor of my brother, but more—more patience and compassion melted together by his burning desire.

In these few weeks, I'd fallen for him in a way I never dreamed possible.

Yet, as life intervened, time together was limited.

Despite—or maybe because of—the dangers that Reid, Patrick, Mr. Sparrow, and my brother all claimed were knocking at our door, any time that Reid and I could spend together was precious.

Reid shifted his weight until we were no longer joined as one. Turning on his side, he lay opposite me, nose to nose. His large hands cupped my cheeks as he brought our lips together.

A moan escaped my lips as his tongue sought entrance. Willingly I opened, welcoming the connection and tasting my own essence. It brought back the memory of how he'd brought me to ecstasy before we'd joined together to find a higher cliff. My breasts pushed against his solid chest as my nipples again tightened.

As he pulled away, a cold chill covered my flesh and I again asked, "What has you so worried?"

"I didn't say I was."

I lifted my head, my pulse running faster as I grew terrified of the answer to the question I was about to pose. "Is it about us? About me?"

Taking a deep breath, Reid sat up, moving his long legs over the edge of the bed. Propping my head on my hand with my elbow on the mattress, I relished the view. While Reid may not have the muscle bulk of Mason, muscle was all he was. There wasn't an ounce of fat as his torso flexed and his biceps bulged. Even his thighs and ass were muscular. I could stare for hours on end.

Statues of Greek and Roman gods had nothing on the man who had stolen my heart and satisfied my body. When we were all together, I found myself envisioning what was hidden beneath his jeans and shirts. Even with the other men present, those images along with memories of what he'd done and was capable of doing had me fidgeting in my chair and dampening my panties.

I reached for his hand as he started to stand. "I'm sorry if it's me."

Reid's smile grew as he turned, taking me in. His gaze raked from my messy red hair all the way to my toes, lingering too long at the places in between. "It's not you, Lorna. Right now, with everything that's happening, the time I get to spend with you are the fucking best minutes of the day."

My skin tingled from the way his eyes had washed over me, and my lips curled into a smile from his words. "Then maybe you don't need to leave yet?"

He splayed his fingers over my stomach, the warmth settling heavily between my legs. It didn't matter that he'd just satisfied me, brought me to the best orgasm twice, seeing him in all his naked perfection only made me want more. "If I don't go, I'll keep you locked in my apartment all night and then what will happen?"

"I'll probably die of too many orgasms."

He grinned. "Is that a fatal ailment?"

"I'm willing to find out." As I spoke, Reid's phone pinged with a text message. "Maybe you could turn that off?"

The clouds of worry returned as he lifted the phone from the bedside stand. "Fuck."

There was something alarming in his tone, in that one word. "Reid? Is everything all right?"

"Shit, get dressed."

Our playful banter was over. His order didn't offer room for questioning.

As he stepped into his blue jeans, slid his feet into shoes, and pulled a soft shirt over his head, I hurriedly dressed, putting on my panties, bra, jeans, and blouse. Before I could make sure everything was in place, Reid had my hand and tugged me toward the front of his apartment. Beyond the bedroom, down the hall, past the empty dining room and into the living room, furnished with a bachelor's necessities—a recliner, side table, and television.

"Wait," I tried to slow a man easily twice my size. "I need my shoes."

He turned, his brown eyes wide. "Lorna, it's Mason."

My heart beat against my chest in double time. "Mason? Is he okay?"

"He thinks you're missing. He's searching for you."

"Fuck," I murmured.

It was then Reid opened the door that led to the common area near the elevator. I wasn't through the door when he called, "Mason."

My feet stilled beside Reid.

Standing at the elevator, phone in hand, was my brother. He spun toward us, his green eyes aflame with genuine concern. The clock stilled. Time forgot to move as Mason scanned Reid and me.

Shit, I hadn't looked in the mirror.

Do I look as freshly fucked as I feel?

I swallowed and stood taller. "Mason, Reid got your text." I prayed my voice sounded calmer than I felt. "I'm good. Didn't mean to worry you."

My brother didn't respond, not to me. His stare was fixed on Reid.

The time that earlier hadn't moved suddenly accelerated. In the moment it took me to blink, Reid had pulled me behind him, and Mason had crossed the room, now standing directly before Reid.

"You fucking dick."

LORNA

The tower - nine years ago

"What the hell are you doing with my sister?" Mason growled as simultaneously, his fist collided with Reid's cheek.

My hands sprang to my lips as I let out a stifled scream. "Stop! Mason, stop."

What happened next was too fast to choreograph.

Reid reached for Mason's elbows.

While I'd thought Reid was all muscle, I was seeing proof of it now.

In an instant, Reid had Mason's arms secured behind his back. His voice lowered to a rumbling snarl as he spoke near Mason's ear. "He'll throw her out. Is that what you want?"

"Fucking let go of me."

"Mason." I leaned down, crouching low and meeting his gaze. "Reid hasn't done anything I didn't want."

With flared nostrils and clenched jaw, my brother closed his eyes momentarily. When he opened his eyes again, he looked back at Reid and spoke through gritted teeth. "Let. Go. Of. Me."

Reid's grip loosened.

Mason stood, shook his arms, and straightened his shoulders. "You," he said, pointing at me, "go in our apartment. Don't come out."

Instead of doing what my brother said, I reached for Reid's arm. "Mason, I'm not a kid."

"I fucking know that."

I stood taller. "Then don't treat me like one. While you weren't looking, I grew up. We're not in some one-room excuse for an apartment. Our mother isn't out turning tricks, forgetting she had kids to feed." The words came even though I knew I should stop. "You don't need to take care of me."

"You're here," Mason said, standing his ground. "I'm taking care of you."

"She's here," Reid interjected, "because you thought it would be best. She was and is capable of taking care of herself."

I looked up at the man before me, the one who had just made love to me, the one defending me, not as a child but as an adult capable of making my own choice.

Before I could respond, Mason spoke, louder than before.

"Is that what you think is best? Do you want her back out there instead of here and safe?"

"No. I want her here—with me, not you."

"With you?" I asked.

Reid looked down, our gazes meeting, and nodded. "It wasn't how I imagined saying it."

Yet before he could say more, Mason was closer to him, so close their chests touched. "You and me, we're not done. We're going to talk."

Finding my voice, I turned to Mason. "It's not up to you."

At the same time, Reid replied, "Mason, I wanted to tell you. There's been too much happening with Allister and Sparrow. The timing didn't seem right—"

"What the actual fuck?" Mason interrupted as his blazing green gaze sent flames from me to Reid and back. "This isn't new? How long?"

Heat came from his stare, similar to a spotlight shining on Reid and me.

I tried to shrug. "This" —I motioned between Reid and me— "...not long." Suddenly, I didn't care about Mason. I remembered Reid's words. He'd said he wanted me with him. When I peered up at him, a smile filled my face. "Although, I think I've wanted it for a long time."

I stepped forward and reached for Mason's hand. "Mace."

"Are you going to tell me to fuck off?" my brother asked. "You're done with me and don't need me anymore."

"No, I'm going to remind you that I'm twenty-six years old."

"I fucking know your age."

"You've done so much for me. It was hard when you left, but" —I looked around the common area that at one time felt foreign— "it was meant to be. This, Mace, is the life you were meant to live. The four of you will rule this city. You will help more people like Missy." His hand twitched in mine, but I held tight. "I'll never be able to thank you enough for all you've done. You even took care of me from overseas. Now it's time to let me live."

"With him?" Mason asked.

"Do you have a better prospect?" Reid's chest puffed as his jaw clenched. "I'm not good enough?"

Mason scanned him up and down. "Fuck no." Letting go of my hand, my brother took a step back before raking his fingers through his short light-brown hair. "Fuck, Reid, this is about my sister. Not about you."

We all grew silent and turned as the elevator doors opened.

I took a deep breath, wishing I could turn back time. Wishing I could be back in Reid's bed, or maybe in the apartment where Mason wanted me. Wishing I was anywhere but here, facing him—Sterling Sparrow.

He didn't need to speak to express his displeasure. It radiated off of him, sending ripples through the air. His deep voice bellowed, echoing through the common area. "Tell me what the fuck is going on."

Patrick appeared a few steps behind in Mr. Sparrow's wake.

When no one replied, Sparrow stopped and scanned from Reid to me and finally to Mason. "Our city is under siege and you two are fighting over *her?*"

The way he said the personal pronoun was the way someone would describe dog shit stuck to their shoe. Whether he meant it or not, I heard the disgust in his tone. This man had chosen his army, but similar to the nation's military, he hadn't issued his soldiers a family.

I wasn't wanted.

Despite Mason's preference or even Reid's, the only person capable of making the decision had just spoken. Taking a deep breath, I straightened my neck and stepped forward. Reid had been right. I was capable of taking care of myself. I didn't need a man—my brother, my lover, or this arrogant asshole. I met Sterling Sparrow's frightening stare with as much strength and dignity as I could muster. Lifting my chin, I said, "I'll pack my things and be gone before the four of you return in the morning."

Before Mr. Sparrow or either of the men beside me could respond, another voice was heard.

"You're staying."

Everyone turned to the man speaking; we turned to Patrick.

"Come on," Patrick said, making eye contact with each of his colleagues. "We have a city to control." He spoke to Mason. "Lorna is your family, Mason." He turned to the man still emanating his displeasure. "Sparrow, you say all the time that we watch out for our own. That includes Lorna. No one in this room will be responsible for her being on the street where there's the possibility of anything happening to her."

"Get her a plane ticket," Sparrow replied. "She can be out of the country by tomorrow. You heard her. She's ready to leave. We can assure her safety in Europe."

Patrick shook his head. "The ultimate decision may be yours, boss. Right now, you're not thinking about family. Your mind's on the fight for control of Chicago as it should be. Give this" —he lifted his hand toward the rest of us— "time. We all have time."

At some point during Patrick's speech, I'd stepped back, wedging myself between Reid and Mason.

Patrick turned his eyes back toward the three of us. "Mason, your family is our family." He smirked as he turned to Reid. "In light of recent developments that sounds a bit gross, but go with me on this. Forget your last names. If we're in this fight, we're all Sparrows.

"The three of you will work out your issues with time. Currently, we have more important things to deal with. McFadden's men are, as we speak, gathering at an abandoned flophouse in East Garfield Park. Shit's happening. We have one man on the inside. Either we'll get the intel or we'll lose a man. Then there's the shipment at the shipyard. I can't get ahold of the capo we sent to investigate. That is where our heads need to be." He gestured between us. "This here—can wait."

We all turned toward Sparrow. With a grunt, he barked to

the men, "Down to 2, now." His dark eyes came to me. "Stay put. You're already too much of a distraction."

I ventured a step away from my brother and my lover and again lifted my chin. My voice was not as strong as before, but I forced myself to speak. "I'll take the ticket if that's what you want."

Mason reached for my hand. "Lorna."

"No," Sparrow said. "You're not going anywhere until things are settled. Just stay out of the way."

I let out my breath, unsure if I was pleased with his change of perspective, or afraid for what would come once things settled.

Would I become accustomed to this odd grouping only to be sent away?

With my hand still in Mason's, I remained silent.

Sparrow scanned the group. "Now, if you have balls, get in the elevator. If you don't, go to bed." Reaching the elevator, he stepped inside.

I looked down to Mace's and my connection, wondering how many times we'd stood together facing a tyrant. The difference was that this tyrant was my brother's friend.

When I looked up, Sparrow, inside the elevator, was holding the door open, his dark stare zeroed in on me. "I mean it," he said. "Stay put. Don't try to leave, the elevators won't work."

Patrick nodded, sending a suggestion of a reassuring smile my way before entering the elevator after Sparrow.

Mason turned to me as he squeezed my hand. "I know you're grown up. It's just..."

I fought tears as they prickled the backs of my eyes and stared up at my lifelong protector. I didn't want to shut him out. I simply wanted more. I wanted Reid too. "Me too, Mace."

As he released my hand and followed the other two men into the elevator, I wondered if I was selfish to want both men in differing roles.

Was I asking too much of the universe?

After all, I was living in a high-rise glass tower above Chicago. Did I deserve more than that?

Before I could contemplate further, Reid reached for my hand and whispered, "It will be okay."

I looked from the way our fingers wove together up into the gaze I'd grown to love. "Do you promise?"

He nodded. "I give you my word, Lorna. Now that the news of us is out, we will make it work." He looked over at the waiting elevator and back to me, keeping his voice low. "Mason is a good guy. He loves you."

I nodded and took a step toward the apartment I'd shared with my brother.

Reid held on to my hand. When I looked up again, he whispered, "And so do I."

I squeezed his hand, unable to respond. I also couldn't watch as Reid walked toward the elevator. Instead, I stepped into Mason's apartment and shut the door behind me. The storm of emotions was overwhelming.

As I leaned against the closed door to the common area, I didn't see the interior of my brother's apartment. I heard the thunder of Mr. Sparrow's voice, the bolts of lightning in my brother's eyes, the calming winds of Patrick's words, and the hope for a future in Reid's declaration of love.

Holding my midsection, I slid downward until I hugged my knees, sitting upon the entryway floor in the nicest place my brother and I had ever lived.

REID

Present day

*M*ason led me down a long a hallway, the walls lined with framed enlarged photographs. On another visit, I'd stopped and examined their beauty. Each one was of something or someplace on the ranch. Whether it was a photograph of a babbling brook, a close-up of a rain-soaked flower, or the panoramic view of a snowcapped mountain with a stunning backdrop of sky filled with pink and purple, the photographs showcased the best of what this terrain had to offer. We were almost to the office door when one of the pictures caught my attention.

"Who took this photo?" I asked, pointing at the black and white aerial view of the ranch.

Mason stopped. "Laurel did...from my plane."

I examined what I could see of the ranch from the height the plane must have been flying. "Is this all of your land?"

"Mostly. Why?"

"Where did they take them?" I turned to Mason. "Do you think they could be on your land?"

Mason's expression fell. "Man, I'm not trying to be negative, but a typical helicopter, if that is what we are dealing with, flies at about 135 knots and can travel three hundred to three hundred and fifty miles before it needs to refuel."

"That makes our circle roughly one hundred and fifty to one hundred and seventy-five miles," I said, "assuming they flew here and back on one tank."

Mason took a step back and raked his fingers through his long hair. "If we're dealing with a typical chopper that would be the case. If my gut is correct, the Order's resources aren't typical. The Lockheed AH-56A Cheyenne can fly twelve hundred miles and go higher." Mason lifted his chin toward the living room. "Some of those mountains out there are as high as thirteen thousand feet."

I thought about what he was saying, unwilling to get distracted. "All right, we have some fucking land to survey. I'll go through your security. Get Sparrow and Patrick on calls with contacts around the country to find out what is happening in their outfits. I need you to create a topographical map with the range of different helicopters. I need coordinates to utilize satellites and get their data."

Mason nodded. "Can you get back data?"

"I'm not sure. Real time is more easily accessible. In Chicago I have everything stored. I can start doing that here, but it won't help for the past. Once I have the security figured out, I'll know what time frame we're talking about and go from there."

"Once we have that data," he replied, "we'll have a better idea of where to send the capos. This fucking land is too open to send them knocking down doors."

My lips came together in a straight line as I considered all that we needed to learn before we could begin to search.

"Let's get started," Mason said.

We stopped at the doorway to the office. It wasn't secure as I'd expected. The door was open, a metal door that slid into the wall, smaller but similar to our floor 2. We both peered inside.

Mason's neck straightened. "This is why we don't let the ladies on 2."

I couldn't stop my grin. Inside the office was a long table that had obviously been taken over by Laurel. There were multiple screens and a keyboard. There were also several laptops, notebooks stacked four to ten high in multiple piles, and glasses of half-empty drinks. From the distance, I identified iced tea, water, and lemonade.

"Wait," I said, "didn't Garrett say Laurel thought it was the lemonade that they believed was drugged?"

Mason's gaze went from the glasses to me. "Yeah." He went toward the glasses. "Fuck."

"Stop. I can dust the glass. It won't be as good as what I

have back in Chicago, but I can run some tests on the contents. Laurel can help."

"We need to be sure there isn't any—"

Mason didn't complete his sentence as he pushed past me and hurried toward the kitchen.

I took a deep breath and looked past the mess on the long table. Beyond was a smaller replication of our Chicago lair. There were even screens mounted high above. Instead of four seats with keyboards, there were only two. I settled at the one that appeared less occupied. Stretching my fingers over the keyboard, I hesitated.

Was there a password?

Surely, it wasn't this easy to access Mason's technology.

I hit one key. The closest screen came to life with a photograph similar to one of the ones in the hallway. In the middle was the place to enter the password. I tried to recall, and then I did. I remembered helping Mason set this up after the explosion that leveled most of his first home.

I gave the password I'd used back then a try.

The screen changed.

I was in.

My fingers began moving. This was what I did, how I computed information. This was my contribution to the Sparrow outfit, maneuvering technology. Time didn't register as I found myself looping through the different programs. I still had the black hole of thirty minutes.

"We have this," Mason said as he re-entered the room, carrying a half-filled jug of lemonade. "Laurel confirmed what

Garrett told Patrick: everyone ate something different for lunch. They all made their own. Sandwiches, salads, fruit, cottage cheese. The only thing that all four of them had was this." He lifted the jug higher.

"And besides you, they all touched the jug?"

"Yes, and Garrett. He brought the groceries into the house a few days ago and put them away."

"Where did he—"

"Lindsey Dorgan," Mason interrupted. "She went to Bozeman to buy a list of groceries Laurel requested."

"She's Seth's wife," I said for confirmation.

"Laurel is confident the jug hadn't been opened before she opened it. There's a seal under the cap, or there was."

I leaned back in the leather chair. "The groceries were bought a few days ago?"

Mason set the jug down on the long table. "Yes." His green gaze narrowed as he stared down at the partially filled jug. "It wasn't this, was it?"

"I'd say no." I stood and walked to the table. "I mean, I could run a pH test on the drink in the jug and this one, but" —I picked up the glass and held it to the light— "this one appears to have melted ice. The jug will have a lower pH." I looked up to Mason. "GHB and similar drugs decrease the pH of the solution once it's added. The problem with lemonade is that the pH is already low."

Mason came closer and took the glass. "I could take a drink to find out."

"You could and if I'm wrong, you'll be sleeping for the

next two to three hours or if you don't fall asleep, you'll not remember anything. I think we have too much shit going on for that kind of an experiment."

He lifted the glass to his mouth, tipped it, and brought a small amount of the liquid to his lips. Once he tipped the glass back, he said, "GHB has a salty taste."

"That's obviously diluted."

He set the glass back on the table. "It doesn't make sense. Whoever took Lorna and Araneae knew the ladies would be unconscious or at least unlikely to remember. How would they know that they drank the lemonade days after it was brought to the house?"

"Unless the drug was just added."

"We need to see who has been in this house."

I sat back down at the keyboard, accessing the security program. There were sensors on each entrance that automatically recorded with movement. A quick scroll and I could see every door that opened or closed and the person there.

"Minus the time still missing, no one other than the ladies or Garrett entered this house today," I said. "Not until us."

"Mason."

We both turned to the doorway to see Sparrow standing there. "Did you get ahold of Seth?"

"Yes." Mason looked at his watch. "He'll have all the field hands in the bunkhouse in another thirty minutes."

"I'm going down there with you. We can get through them faster if we both ask questions. And this is your property."

Mason nodded. "What about Patrick?"

"He's in your study contacting other outfits around the country. He's already spoken to Carlos Perez from Denver, and I reached out to Sasha Bykov in Detroit. They had nothing significant to report. Without giving them too much information, we warned them to be extra vigilant."

Mason walked to the other keyboard and began typing. "Here's the map of the ranch and beyond," he said. "I can get a paper map too."

"We could use that later," Sparrow said. He looked at me. "I know you don't want to, but go up to your suite, Lorna's, soon."

My gaze narrowed. "Why?"

Sadness seeped from his being. "Just do it. I went up and took a look around. Granted, I don't know every fucking purse Araneae carries, but the one with all her things is upstairs in the closet."

"Fuck," I muttered. "Sorry, I could confirm that by checking the trackers."

"Yeah," he said, "I guess I wanted to see." He turned to Mason. "It definitely was a helicopter. Back behind the building where we are going to house the capos, you can see how the blades blew the tall grass."

"You went out there?" Mason asked.

"Yes. Patrick and I were looking at the building you mentioned."

I recalled Mason's concern. "Can we get a good print on the landing skids?"

"Not perfect, but close," Sparrow replied.

Mason looked at me. "I'll go out there and measure their length before we head down to the bunkhouse." He looked to Sparrow. "It will probably be dark by the time we get back."

Sparrow nodded. "I'm ready to start doing something."

Mason turned to me. "You good?"

"No," I replied honestly. "But this" —I lifted my chin to the screens— "is what I do. It makes me feel like I'm doing something."

"I'll text you with the measurements on the skids. Text or call if you learn something."

"What about the capos?"

"Patrick is on that," Sparrow replied.

Mason's large hand slapped my shoulder. "We're getting them back."

"What about ransom?" Sparrow asked. "We haven't heard anything."

"We need to keep all lines of communication open," I said.

After both men left, I began scanning the three different security programs we'd combined. Mason was right about one thing: it would take someone with a higher understanding of security to override this system. Hitting a few keys, I created a visual readout of the three programs and ran them in parallel format. I continued working, narrowing down the exact time of the breach to within seven minutes.

"Reid," Laurel said from the doorway with a plate in her hand. She forced a smile. "It's late. I brought you some dinner."

Dinner?

I turned to the clock on the screen. It was nearly eight thirty, which was nine thirty in Chicago, and yet I wasn't hungry. I'd been too consumed with what I had been doing. It also didn't help that the office was windowless.

She carried the plate closer and placed it and a fork wrapped in a napkin on the desk beside the keyboard and my notes. From a pocket in her oversized sweater, she pulled out a water bottle. "Still sealed." When I didn't respond, she added, "I know what it's like to get lost in your work."

I looked at the long table. "Laurel, this is your house. You don't have to leave me alone if you have work you want to do."

"I have a lot I want to do. Right now, I'd do anything to help you find Lorna and Araneae."

The sight of the food returned my stomach to life. "It looks delicious."

"I don't profess to have the culinary skills of your wife."

I grinned. "I don't think many can."

"Was she always a good cook?" Laurel asked.

I thought back to when Lorna and I were first married. Hell, we hadn't known one another that long. I could say we were in love. I think I was. I think she was. It was a difficult time, and I knew I'd do anything to keep her safe. Cooking was something she wanted to do. Hell, before her, the four of us lived on takeout and packaged meals. Anything was an improvement over that.

The memories brought on an unexpected and needed smile.

"If I tell you the truth, you have to promise you'll tell her what I say when we have her home."

"You want me to tell?" Laurel asked as she turned a chair toward me and took a seat at the long table.

"I do." I imagined my wife's smile, the way her green eyes could tell an entire story, and how she could communicate without saying a word. "Lorna and I have always been painfully honest with one another." I shrugged. "There are things—Sparrow things—that I can't share, but I've never lied to her. Besides, I love seeing the fiery smirk in her green eyes. And if you tell her what I'm about to say, which is that with the exception of a few dishes, Lorna was a pitiful cook, while it's the God's honest truth, my wife will most definitely give me *that* look."

"Pitiful? Really?"

"Chicken Parmesan has always been her specialty. Her recipe was her grandmother's. That's something we had in common, our love of our grandmothers."

Laurel hummed. "I love her chicken Parmesan."

As we spoke and I started to eat, the program I'd been running caught my attention. The seven-minute gap was down to two. It was working. The layers were starting to fill one another in.

"What is it?" Laurel asked, standing and coming near, peering over my shoulder at the screen.

"I fucking hope it's our answer."

LORNA

*T*he food we'd been fed churned in my stomach, sloshing with the water, as I paced the length of the cell and back. I'd lost count of how many times I'd made the trek or the number of the steps it took to get from one side of the room to the other. I'd also lost track of time.

Had night come and gone?

Was this the next day?

Was it still the same, never-ending nightmare?

More than once, I'd fallen to my knees in front of the toilet attached to the wall near a small sink, certain I was about to vomit the contents of my stomach. If it was possible that stubbornness could keep the bile and food from moving upward, I had it in spades.

I would not give up the small bit of nutrients because if I

did, I would be helpless to fight for the return of what else I'd lost...one of my best friends.

Hours ago~

After securing our blindfolds, Araneae and I waited in the frightening darkness. Loss of sight amplified the other senses. The lingering scent of our tasteless meal hung heavily in the air and upon my tongue. The rough texture of the blindfold abraded my face as Araneae's grip of my hand grew tighter. A cool breeze, before undetectable, blew over my arms, bringing goose bumps to life. Beyond the edges of my blindfold, light saturated the room.

All of those sensations paled in comparison to hearing, that sense now on overdrive. As if someone had just turned up the volume, the ordinarily minute sounds roared. My pulse thundered in my ears like a violent Chicago storm. The rapid breaths from both Araneae and I filled the air like gusts of wind before tornadic activity.

The atmosphere around us shifted as the door's lock clicked, activating the internal mechanism. The turning knob and scratch of the door's bottom over the concrete floor preceded heavy footsteps. The pungent scent of body odor made me flinch.

Beneath my blindfold I once again saw the boots and jeans from before.

"You." The pronoun was the only directive from the deep voice.

My nerves grew tauter as I waited for more.

Who was you?

I shifted, wondering if it was me. As I did, Araneae's grasp of my hand loosened.

"Wait, what's happening?" I asked to the darkness.

"I'll be fine," Araneae said, her voice stronger than I could have mustered. "I'll walk. Please don't touch me."

"No," I called, pushing myself off the bunk. I lifted my chin in time to see the man's legs covered in jeans and his boot-clad feet moving beside Araneae's legs and bare feet. "Don't take her without me."

My plea echoed in the small cell, a lingering cry as Araneae was taken away. I ripped the blindfold from my eyes in time to see the door click shut. I ran toward it, pulling on the knob. It wiggled in my grip, but not enough to activate the latch.

"No, please," I called to whoever could hear.

My hands balled to fists as I pounded on the solid metal— pound after pound until my hands bruised and tears fell from my eyes. "She's pregnant," I cried as too many visions came to mind. "Please don't hurt her. Don't hurt the baby."

No one answered.

There was no one to respond.

I was alone.

I spun around, taking in the cell where we'd been placed, thinking about the reality. This was a lockdown. My experiences back in the tower in no way prepared me for this isolation. When there, I'd had space—Mason's apartment, Reid's apartment, the first floor of the penthouse. What I'd considered solitary was a beautiful big home compared to where I was now.

Completely alone.

That wasn't quite accurate.

I recognized my companion. It was one I'd known for most of my life. Its name varied, but most people called it fear —that sensation that surpassed the normal senses and burrowed under the skin. As a little girl, I felt it lurking in the shadowy corners, taking residence under my bed and chilling my skin as a warning.

Was that what it was doing now?

Was my companion warning me?

My skin prickled as I again turned completely around. There were no dark corners to keep it hidden. I crouched down, peering under the bunk bed, and lifted my chin upward, searching in the rafters near the burning light bulbs. I couldn't see it, but that didn't matter. It was here, a master at disguise.

No longer was I fearful of one of my mother's johns, or an odd man on the L. Today there was nothing as obvious, yet it existed all around me, an invisible force capable of mass destruction. Its presence was in every fiber of my being. Even as the tears dried and my stomach calmed, fear remained.

. . .

Present time-

I couldn't lie upon the thin, cot-like mattress. Before our dinner arrived, Araneae and I decided that I would sleep on the high one. It made sense for her not to climb. Truly her baby bump wasn't big enough to be a hindrance; it was the principle of the thing. A pregnant woman didn't need to climb.

Of course, I'd never made it up to the top bunk. We'd sat together on the lower bunk, our backs against the wall, finding comfort in one another's company. My mind swirled with possibilities.

Maybe they discovered who she was, the founder of the Sparrow Institute, co-owner of Sinful Threads—a successful fashion company, and most significantly, the wife of Sterling Sparrow.

I tried to reassure myself that Araneae was safe and on her way back to Chicago or Mason's ranch. If our kidnappers knew both of our identities, keeping just one of us would be enough. Reid and I were more than financially secure. He would pay generously for my return. He wasn't the only one. I had no doubt that Sparrow would pay too.

There was a time when he didn't want me around.

It was past.

We'd worked through the obstacles, leaving our friendship stronger.

My breathing caught as the light disappeared.

With trembling hands, I hurriedly secured my blindfold as my pulse thumped again in my ears, my breathing reverberating against the cement-block walls. I held on to the metal frame of the bunk bed as the locking mechanisms in the door clicked and finally, the bottom of the door scooted across the floor.

I strained to see what was hidden, to smell what hadn't yet registered, to feel a familiar touch, and to hear what was still out of range. And then I heard.

REID

$\mathcal{I}$ pointed at the large paper topographical map of Mason's property lying upon his dining room table. "We need to verify that the helicopter left the ranch's property."

The hums of my colleagues filled the air.

Although it was nearly midnight, we were all together in a room with a table large enough to hold the surveys and maps. The dining room's long wall of windows that during the day offered a stunning view, now peered out at the beginning of a moonless night. With the combination of latitude and longitude, the hours of daylight here at the ranch were much longer in the summertime than in Chicago. Even so, the sun had recently given up the ghost, giving way to a lingering dusk.

The suspended day and delayed night created an eerie and unsettling sensation.

It felt as if we were on the brink of a black hole—a loss of time and space that once we crossed over, we'd never return. The unspoken restlessness was evident in our murmurs and seen in the strained features of our expressions. The four of us were tried-and-true soldiers. We'd fought enemies and conquered cities. We'd also experienced loss. The latter was the catalyst that kept us focused, kept us going.

The warm breeze blowing from the open windows, doors, and overhead fans rustled the maps. Patrick and Mason hurriedly rearranged empty coffee cups whose new job now was acting as paperweights.

"Tomorrow the equipment will arrive to clean the ducts," Mason said as he rescued a flyaway note one of us had written earlier.

This wasn't the only room. All the windows were open throughout the house. Capos were stationed conspicuously around the exterior perimeter. The house was opened to the world, but no one was getting close.

"I'm going to bed," Laurel said as she entered the room, her long sweater wrapped around her body, covering her long pants, top, and nearly down to her sock-covered feet.

"We'll get this secure tomorrow," Mason reassured her.

"I really thought it was the lemonade."

"Whatever they added to the ventilation system worked fast," Patrick said.

"But Madeline..." Laurel began.

Patrick shrugged. "She was tired, as she suspected. According to the information Reid recovered, Maddie was already up in our room before the knockout gas agent was activated."

Laurel shook her head. "I wish I hadn't left the other two in the kitchen."

Sparrow looked up from the maps he'd been studying. "Don't do that, Laurel."

"I just..." She let her words trail away.

He stood tall and stretched his shoulders and neck. "Go to bed. We need your help tomorrow in determining the agent that was used. The canister is bagged. If you'd been in the kitchen, you wouldn't be here to help us now."

Her blue eyes veered to her husband. From my angle I couldn't read their unspoken message. If I were to guess, it would be survivor's remorse. Laurel didn't need to bear that. Lorna and Araneae would survive this. I couldn't allow myself to think otherwise.

Mason wrapped his arm around his wife's waist and laid a kiss on the top of her hair. "I don't know when—"

Laurel shook her head. "Do whatever you need to do." She turned toward the rest of us. "All of you, do what you do. I'm sorry my work is cluttering the table in the office. I'll clean it up tomorrow and take it upstairs. As for now, Madeline is asleep, and I'm going upstairs. No one will disturb you."

Sparrow and I nodded while Patrick added his *good nights* to Mason's.

Once Laurel was gone, Sparrow spoke, his focus back on our discoveries. "We know the helicopter headed west."

"Based on the size of the landing skids," Mason began, "we're looking at the possibility that the chopper could fly roughly three to four hundred miles on a full tank."

"There's no reason to think the tank was full. It flew here," Patrick replied.

"But we don't know from where," Mason added. "It could have refueled as close as Bozeman before coming here. Reid is running a program to check the closest fueling stations."

"Or on your property," Patrick countered. "If the kidnappers weren't working alone, one man with a pickup truck and cans of fuel could refuel a helicopter." He took a deep breath. "This is all theoretically sound, but logistically, there are too many variables."

It was our ongoing conversation. An idea would come and three would counter. We weren't arguing as much as brainstorming, narrowing possibilities, and eliminating the improbable.

I looked up from the laptop where I was currently working. "No flight plans were filed anywhere with coordinates that come close to your property." Before anyone could respond, I added, "I didn't expect there to be, but I had to check."

Mason went to the open window and looked out into the growing darkness. "According to the FAA, private planes or helicopters flying under eighteen thousand feet don't require a flight plan." He tilted his chin toward the cooling darkness. "Even the highest peaks are under that range."

"Right," I said, "yet a helicopter landed." I gave it a second thought. "What are the chances anyone noticed?"

"High," Mason said. "A low-flying helicopter would be an oddity. Yet, none of the ranch hands saw it. Sparrow and I questioned every one of them. They'd been repairing fences in pasture seven, northeast of here."

"And no one heard or saw a fucking thing," Sparrow said.

None of the ranch hands had, but Lindsey Dorgan and her eight-year-old son did. They'd been tending some newly acquired horses a few pastures over. Her son heard the helicopter first. Neither of them realized it had landed, but we had the confirmation we needed. Then the information I found on the security video made it official.

Sparrow tilted his chin toward the table. "I want to see a broader map. I want to know every dwelling within a three-hundred-mile radius of this house."

I began to type upon the keyboard. As the search engine spun, my nerves grew taut. "I need faster fucking service."

Everyone's eyes turned my direction.

"It's all right, Reid," Patrick said. "We have a fuck more questions than answers."

"We know they were taken," I said, waiting for the program to load, "around one o'clock, nearly twelve hours ago. The colorless, odorless agent, commonly referred to as knockout gas, began filtering through the ventilation system at the top of the hour. When the two kidnappers entered through the doors on the balcony off the kitchen, every one of the women was already unconscious." I stood and began pacing. "The two kidnappers are most likely men based on their build. There's no way to run facial recognition because they were wearing gas masks."

"Which means," Patrick added, "they knew about the agent."

Sparrow leaned against the wall near the windows that opened to the same balcony where the kidnappers entered. He crossed his arms over his chest. While Laurel had been bundled in a sweater, long pants, and socks, with the open windows and doors, Sparrow, like the rest of us was wearing jeans and short sleeves, perceivably unaffected by the cooling air. "This was planned."

I nodded. "But when? I haven't been able to determine when the canister was placed."

"Fuck," Mason said. "It could have been there for a while, waiting for the right time."

I looked at Mason. "How? How was someone not detected placing it?"

"The fucking house sits empty more than it's occupied." He took a deep breath and turned my way. "But you're right. We have no way of knowing when. We need to go back and search for missing time. It wouldn't have taken long to place."

"No," Sparrow said as he stepped away from the wall. "One day I'll give a fuck about when the canister was planted. Today isn't that day. We're done looking back. We need to proceed with looking forward. The ducts have been searched thoroughly. We know there aren't more. Right now, we need to determine who masterminded this in advance, who placed the canister, who activated it, and why. We also, and more importantly, need to get Araneae and Lorna home." His muscles pulled tight, veins and tendons popping to life in his neck. "Give me a goddamned ransom. I'll pay, and then I'll make fucking sure the kidnappers suffer for touching my family."

The program I'd started was responding. "What kind of dwellings are we looking for?" I asked as I began to set the perimeters on the search.

Sparrow and Mason began spewing specifics—abandoned storefronts, warehouses, barns...

"Tomorrow," Mason said, "we can take my plane up. It only holds one other passenger. We can do a visual of this property and the neighboring properties."

"Something is bothering me," Patrick said as he stared at the maps.

"Just one thing?" I asked.

He turned to me. "Can you, with confidence, say the canister that was found was not placed today prior to the kidnapping?"

"One hundred percent," I replied.

"In the last week?"

"I need to do some more searches, but yes. The only missing time since we arrived on this ranch with the ladies was the missing time earlier today."

Patrick looked at Mason. "They weren't after Araneae and Lorna. You were the target."

Mason's eyes closed and opened before he slowly nodded.

"But," Patrick interjected, "think about it. They took two women. They had to know you weren't one of them."

My heart began to beat faster. "Unless you weren't the target," I said to Mason as I stood. "Not you, but..."

"Laurel," we all said together.

LORNA

$\mathcal{M}$y grasp of the metal frame tightened, and I willed my pulse to calm as heavy footsteps entered the cell. My mind told me to tip my chin upward and try to see but to see what? I'd already seen the jeans and boots, and the slacks and shoes. My breath caught in my chest as the stale stench returned, the footsteps stilled, and the bunk bed shook.

Before I could speak, the sound of moaning filled the cell.

"Araneae?"

The footsteps moved toward the door, their bearer void of any explanation. It didn't take long, a second or less, till it closed and the locking mechanism clicked. My breath came forward in a gust as I ripped the blindfold from my eyes and saw my friend lying upon the bottom bunk. "Araneae."

She didn't speak as I moved to her. Her eyes were closed,

and her knees drawn upward. Her hands were over her midsection as her facial features contorted. Her skin glistened with perspiration.

I sat on the edge of the bunk and gently smoothed her long blonde hair away from her face. "Araneae, I'm here. It's Lorna."

Her head moved ever so slightly from side to side, yet she didn't utter a word.

I began to scan from her head to her toes, taking in any exposed skin. While contorted in an unusual way, her face was clear of abuse. There were no reddened areas, bruises, or lacerations. As I continued to smooth her hair and speak softly, tears fell from her closed eyes, like small streams, making their way to the pillow beneath her head.

"What happened?" I asked. "Did they hurt you?"

Her presence combined with silence was more deafening than when I'd been alone.

It was then I noticed the two water bottles lying upon the floor near the door. I hadn't heard them as they were dropped, but my attention had been on the man's steps and the squeak coming from the bunk bed as he'd laid Araneae down.

I hurried to gather the bottles and brought them back to the bunk bed. In the split second I'd been gone, Araneae had begun to shiver. Instead of struggling with the covers she was lying upon, I returned the bottles again to the floor, reached for the covers on the top bunk, and pulled the thin blanket from the mattress. Next, I covered her from her chin to her toes, tucking the edges around her to help retain her warmth. Through it all, her eyes stayed closed.

Her expression had eased as if she had fallen into a much-needed sleep. I wanted to tell myself that was all that this was. Araneae was exhausted and to combat that state, her body needed sleep.

Next, I pulled the top bunk pillow down and moved her into a more inclined position. The last thing I tried was the water. After first ensuring that the bottles had been sealed, I opened one and brought the spout to her mouth. "Come on, Araneae. You need to drink."

I tilted the bottle until the liquid reached her lips. That was as far as it went. She didn't move or acknowledge my assistance. The water flowed from her lips down her chin.

"It's all right," I soothed as I sopped it with the blanket. "Sleep first and drink later."

Though her skin felt warm, her body trembled beneath the blanket. Getting up, I went to the sink and saturated a thin washcloth with cold water from the faucet. Squeezing out the excess, I folded the cloth and took it back to Araneae. I placed it on her forehead and looked around our cell. The supplies were limited at best.

Unsure what else to do with what I had, I took a small sip of the water, wanting to save most if it for her, and again sat on the mattress beside her. After a few minutes, I stretched out on the few inches of space beside her. With my head next to hers on the pillow, I wrapped one arm over her and softly spoke.

"Do you remember the first time we met?" Though she didn't respond, I imagined her voice full of zeal and joy. I pretended to hear her determination in the way she voiced her power as queen of Chicago.

"I do," I said, "like I've said several times, I was nervous about your arrival, and then when you did arrive, you were like you are now." I took a ragged breath. "No, you were unconscious, but then it was because someone tried to hurt you. Now, you're only tired."

I worked to slow my breathing. "That first morning, Sparrow carried you down to the kitchen." I smirked at the memory. "He was all caveman. Even though you were weak from whatever had happened, you were still strong and spunky. In only a few minutes, my worries about you disappeared. And then later that day, you called me. He'd left strict instructions that you were to remain upstairs." My smile grew bigger. "But he forgot to inform you of his supreme authoritarian power. Or..." I turned toward Araneae, saw her closed eyes, and heard her even breaths. "Or maybe you didn't care. Maybe you already knew you had him wrapped around your little finger." I moved my hand down, momentarily over her midsection. "Just like this baby will. If she's a girl, God help us. Sparrow is a goner. If he's a boy, he'll need you to be the mom Sparrow never had." I looked back at her closed eyes. "Anyway, on with my story, you wanted your laptop.

"Gosh, that was three years ago, and I remember it like it was yesterday. I'm not sure Sparrow knew. No, I'm sure he didn't. I think we told you...a little, but the truth was that all of us—Reid, Patrick, and I—we were all rooting for you. We were on your side from day one, even though we knew Sparrow better. It wasn't that we were rooting against him." I tried to articulate my thoughts. "It was that you were and are who is best for him.

"You see, there have only really been two people that I know of who can dish shit out to your husband unfiltered and get away with it."

I thought back to the very beginning, to nine years ago.

"I never knew his father, the man who ran Sparrow Enterprises and the Sparrow we're not supposed to talk about, before Sterling..." I let his name hang in the air. While Madeline and Laurel called him by his first name, I was of the old group. To me he was Sparrow. "I don't know how his father talked to him." I rolled on my back and stared up at the top bunk. "I know his mother." My voice grew a bit louder. "You are not what she had planned. And that may be another reason we're all on your side.

"But as I was saying, two people...Mason was and is one. But after Mason..." I swallowed. "...left us for a while, there wasn't anyone who threw shit back at him. Patrick is all about diplomacy. He will disagree with Sparrow, but he does it in a way that is nonconfrontational. Reid is usually quiet. He isn't against voicing his opinion when necessary, but it isn't the way Mace does." I turned back to her. "Or you."

I lay still for a moment, my mind filling with memories, ones that took me away from this cool cell.

"The elevator. We weren't joking. Reid, Patrick, and I had a bet going."

Araneae moved her head from side to side. "No..." The word was barely audible.

I sat upward. "Araneae."

Her face was again in a grimace, but there were no more movements or sounds.

Suddenly, I considered what could have happened to her in the hours she was out of this room. Despite her chill, I stood and peeled back the blanket that I'd wrapped around her. My mind and body cooled with fear of what I'd discover.

Who had us captive?

What kind of an animal would hurt a pregnant woman?

Even if someone could forget her affiliation with Sterling Sparrow, she was carrying a child within her.

I held my breath as I scanned her now-prone body—no longer were her knees pulled up. Taking a deep breath, I lifted the bottom hem of her shirt. Her soft pants came to the middle of her baby bump. Her bra was in place. Nothing looked abnormal.

"Araneae, I'm going to turn you."

If only she would have protested. She didn't.

Closing my eyes, I said a prayer to the God my grandmother served. She daily talked to him in prayer. Now it was my turn. I asked him for a miracle. I asked him to keep Araneae and her child safe. I even offered him a payment in return.

With my eyes still closed, I tilted my chin upward and

spoke in a whisper. "Keep her baby safe, and I don't need to ever have my own."

The offer was said. I couldn't take it back. I wouldn't because I meant it.

With the new pregnancies in our extended family, Reid and I had discussed the subject, one that had never been on the table in the past. To my surprise, we were both willing and excited. I thought of the sister I helped raise, the one we'd lost. I found myself thinking about my own child.

Each month I told myself it took time for the birth control to get out of my system. And yet with Madeline's news, and then Araneae's, I still felt joy like I couldn't describe.

Yes, I would offer my future children to keep this one safe. I'd do the same for Madeline and Patrick's. Without a doubt, I'd do the same for Ruby.

Opening my eyes, I moved my friend, fearful of what I'd find. As I turned her on her side, I exhaled. The blood I'd feared I'd find was nonexistent.

She moaned as she settled on her side, facing the wall.

I covered her again with the blanket and climbed back onto the bed. With my pulse thumping in my ears, I whispered, "We can rest now. But since I gave you my blanket and pillow, you're going to have to put up with me."

After taking another swig of the water, I closed my eyes. My emotions counterbalanced one another. I'd meant what I said. I'd give up my future children to keep Araneae's child safe. I wasn't certain God was in the dealmaking business.

If he was, I'd keep my word.

"I have one additional request," I whispered to the Supreme Being. "Please get us home."

With my arm again around my friend, I finally drifted off to sleep.

LORNA

The tower – nine years ago

I looked around Mason's apartment with a heavy heart. It seemed impossible that after spending most of our lives together, there were still too many things we'd left unsaid. For the last week, since I'd learned of my brother's death, I'd cried more tears than I knew were possible. I'd spent long nights and endless days, grieving and also going through his things as more tears streamed down my cheeks.

Probably the most difficult was the trip to the coroner. I don't know if I could have made it alone. I do know. I wouldn't have made it. I wouldn't have stayed upright without the support of his friends. Reid was there, holding my hand. Patrick was there, a steady shoulder to take my tears. Even

Mr. Sparrow was there, silently emanating his remorse and growing need for vengeance.

Mason's body was unidentifiable.

The man I'd known since my first breath was no longer who I remembered.

The story I'd heard about the explosion that took my brother made him out to be the hero he'd always been to me. He walked into a building near the docks because the Sparrows had received a call about a shipment.

Before this incident, I didn't really know what the Sparrows did or what their quest involved.

This was different. Reid decided I deserved more. He told me the details he'd learned from Sparrow. The call said there was a shipment of young girls. Yes, human beings. I wasn't naive enough to live as a single woman and not understand or comprehend the dangers of human trafficking. I'd heard rumors and taken precautions. As I aged, I wondered about my sister's fate.

Had she at one time been a young girl in a shipment?

Mason didn't enter the building to move the girls along the franchise line. He went in that building to rescue them. From Reid's recollection, Sparrow wanted to do it himself. It was Mason who refused to let him. The only man to tell Sparrow no, he'd used that power. He'd saved the kingpin of Chicago and solidified the Sparrow takeover.

In the process, the building exploded.

Reid said that Sparrow ran in.

He didn't need to tell me that detail. I saw the burns on

his hands and the scorched flesh on his cheeks. I saw the eyebrows and eyelashes that were just now beginning to grow back. His visible wounds were superficial: his heart and mindset were where the true battle injuries occurred.

From what I'd heard, I wasn't prepared for the body we were shown in the morgue.

The burns weren't like Sparrow's. Mason's were extensive.

In the mass destruction, I found solace in the knowledge that he passed quickly.

I couldn't comprehend the pain that would be involved in surviving.

The personal possessions I was given sealed his identity. They were undeniably Mason's.

Sparrow left the next decision to me.

What was I to do with the boy turned man who had always been my rock, my lifelong confidant, and my sibling?

Through Reid, I was told no expense would be spared. I was also informed about the explosion, the coup, and the trafficking. I couldn't be responsible for putting my brother's best friends on display. There would be no celebration of life, no military salute, no funeral, and no burial with a headstone. While my brother deserved all of those, the war in Chicago was still in motion. I chose instead to have my brother cremated.

The urn was small, but it was something.

It was more than I had of Missy.

Nothing was said about my place in this world now that I was without Mason.

And while Reid had been loving and supportive, we were never alone. Mason was always there, glaring at us as he had the night he died, the last night Reid and I made love, and the night I learned what Sparrow meant when he said to not go anywhere.

The elevators won't work.

The celebration of life wasn't necessary. Besides the men in this tower, there was only one other person I felt the need to inform of my brother's demise.

It wasn't our mother.

Hell, I wasn't sure she hadn't preceded her son in death. If she hadn't, I had no way of contacting her.

There was one person, someone whom Mason had loved a long time ago. I hadn't thought of her in years until I found a box of letters he'd never bothered to mail. It seemed that for all of my brother's toughness and aloofness, he had a soft spot for a girl from our childhood. Her father volunteered at a Boys and Girls Club near our apartment. He was a doctor and counselor, and always supportive. She was a blue-eyed girl who came from much more than we had. Yet she never acted that way. She was always kind. There was a time I considered her a friend. And then life happened.

Mason went off to the army, Laurel went to college, our mother left for the final time, and I moved on.

Yesterday, using the information on the last letter Mason had written, I asked Reid to help me find her current address. She lived in Indiana, not far and yet a lifetime away. I wrote the only letter to tell anyone about Mason's death. I didn't share details, only that he was gone and he'd never forgotten her. I hesitated but then decided to sign my name.

Reid promised the correspondence would get delivered. He said the USPS was too risky. He didn't want to take the chance that I could be found. What he didn't know was that I wouldn't. I'd soon be gone.

I woke three days ago to an airline ticket and information on an apartment in Stratford-upon-Avon, England. Being the birthplace of William Shakespeare, it was a tourist town, one where I was sure to be able to find a job. I could clean bed and breakfasts or wait tables. My apartment was paid in full for a year and along with the airline ticket, there was an envelope filled with over a thousand of both American dollars and British pounds. There was also information to a bank account in my name, in Warwick, with fifty thousand pounds.

Though the rest was up to me, I wasn't given much choice.

The ticket and information came with a note containing the most words Mr. Sparrow had spared me—ever. He asked me to not share my plans with anyone. He said this arrangement would keep me safe, as Mason had wanted. Those words broke my heart and at the same time, offered me a future, one free of the baggage of my life.

In England, I would be me. I wouldn't be a sister or a daughter. I wouldn't be a secret lover or a distraction. As the last seventy-two hours played out, I told myself that I was thankful Mr. Sparrow had chosen a country with a language I could understand.

Mason was the one born with an uncanny ability with languages and linguistics, not me.

My plane was set to leave in five hours.

My ticket was first class.

And I was to meet a car in two hours.

While I didn't own luggage, Mason did. I believe he'd used it to return from his third tour. Truly, it wasn't much, but it was capable of holding my meager belongings. Those suitcases were now packed as I made another trek around the apartment, determined to take whatever I could to keep my brother with me. Maybe one day he'd stop glaring and instead, I'd see his green eyes and shining smile.

As I checked my purse for the one hundredth time for my ticket and all Mr. Sparrow had given me, there was a knock on Mason's door.

There were only two people who could be on the other side of the door. Mr. Sparrow wasn't an option; he'd said his piece in the form of my eviction notice. That wasn't fair. He wasn't sending me to the street. He'd been extremely generous in his offer.

How could I not take it?

That left the possibilities of Reid or Patrick.

As tears prickled the backs of my eyes, I prayed it was Patrick. I'd already said goodbye to Reid, without letting him know I was. I didn't think my heart could take an encore.

The knock came again.

"Lorna, I know you're in there. Open the damn door."

I took a haggard breath as Reid's deep baritone voice filtered through the door.

"I will fucking break down the damn door."

He sounded—angry?

I had never heard that tone from him before.

My gaze went to the three suitcases lined along the breakfast bar.

The knock turned to pounding.

"Damn it, Lorna. This is your last warning."

Leaving the suitcases where they were, I straightened my neck and shoulders, lifted my chin, and walked to the door. Opening it only enough to catch sight of the man I'd deemed my prince, I feigned strength and resilience I didn't possess. "Reid, what is it?"

It was then I saw as well as heard.

His handsome features were transformed. His soft, loving stare was wild with emotions. The muscles in his neck were taut, and his teeth strained under the immense pressure as his chiseled jaw clenched.

Before he could answer, I took a step back. "Reid?" I'd never seen him as anything other than loving and kind.

He walked past me into the apartment, as he scanned the living room. His dark gaze landed on the suitcases before he spun, seizing my shoulders. "What the actual fuck?" My body shook with his words as his grip upon me intensified. "I was right. You're leaving? You're fucking leaving."

The last statement was no longer in question.

"Stop." I tried to pry myself from his grasp. "Reid..." I

looked up at him and into his dark stare churning with anger. In that second, I was unable to match his rage. I didn't have it in me. What I had was the immense sadness the last week had given me. It no longer simmered but boiled like a raging river trembling through my body. The tears I'd shed in the prior days were nothing in comparison to the gut-wrenching, salty, acidic sobs that sprang like a geyser from the bubbling pool of my emotions.

I'd opened the door ready to fight, but with my body in his grasp, I had none.

The realization hit.

I didn't have the fight.

I had nothing.

Yes, I had suitcases, an airline ticket, money, and a waiting apartment. Compared to what I'd had a week ago with my brother, a lover, and friends, it was nothing, and nothing was my future.

"I-I," I stuttered as my chin fell to my chest.

Reid's large hands released my shoulders. Before I could fall, he gently palmed my cheeks and lifted my bloodshot eyes to his.

We were at a crossroad.

I expected many things.

Reid would yell, as Mason sometimes did.

He would lash out, as men my mother dated had.

He would curse and demand things I wasn't able or willing to give.

I steeled myself for any of those scenarios.

Though I wasn't certain how I would respond, I knew I had to. I had to do as Mr. Sparrow bid. No one other than Mason had crossed him. I sure as hell, at five feet two and one hundred and ten pounds, with no money, no army, and no one on my side, wasn't a formidable opponent against the kingpin of Chicago.

Only my ragged breaths filled my ears until I became aware that I wasn't the only one struggling. This mountain of a beautiful man before me was too. His breaths matched mine. It was as if we'd run a marathon or more enjoyably, both experienced the best sexual experience of our lives.

Neither of those had occurred.

His pain was palpable. It slithered like a snake from him to me. The poisonous venom reminded me that I wasn't the only one to experience loss.

"Reid—"

LORNA

The tower – nine years ago

"*R*eid—?"

One of his hands left my cheek as his finger came to my lips, stopping my words. "No, Lorna, I came here to say something." He took a deep breath, flaring his nostrils and standing taller. "Tell me why you're leaving?"

A question.

I wasn't expecting a question.

My shoulders moved in a shrug as I tried to articulate my plans without saying what Mr. Sparrow had forbidden me to say. "I don't belong here."

Letting go of me, Reid took a step back. His wide chest heaved, stretching the material of his shirt with pent-up breath. His mahogany biceps bulged beneath the sleeves, and his long legs moved slowly around Mason's living room. Finally, he turned, his chin raised high and resolute. "You're right."

He moved toward my suitcases and reached for a handle.

My head shook. "What are you doing?" My volume rose. "You're helping to throw me out?"

He didn't say a word as his dark gaze consumed me. Instead, he reached for the second and then the third suitcase. Lifting all three, he walked toward the door.

As he set down one and opened the door, I found my anger. I found the emotion my sadness had dwarfed. It came back with a vengeance, fueling me like I hadn't been fueled since Mason disappeared in the same elevator I would be leaving in. "Fuck you, Reid. Fuck all of you. You pretended to like me, to care about me. Well, congratulations. You fooled me. And you know what else?" My voice rose, each statement gaining strength.

I was a locomotive heading downhill. I would probably crash at the bottom, but right now I was picking up speed.

He didn't answer as he lifted the suitcases and stepped through the threshold into the common area.

I quickly followed. "Because of you, my last memory of my brother is his hurt. My last..." The damn tears were back. "I'd deceived him. We had trust, he and I, and because of you—"

In the middle of the common area, Reid dropped all of the luggage to the floor and turned. The fire was back in his eyes, blazing out of control. "Because of me?" He came closer.

"Sure, Lorna. If it will make it easier for you to sleep at night, I'll take the blame. I'll take it all." His hands were again on my shoulders, his grip intensifying with every word, to the point of pain. "I'm not going to argue with you over whose decision it was to keep our relationship a secret from Mason. Blame me. I can fucking take it."

"Relationship?" I yelled. "A screw? A piece of meat? What was I exactly to you, Reid? Was it a thrill to know you were banging your friend's sister?"

One hand left my shoulder as it simultaneously gripped my chin. His breathing deepened as strain showed in his taut features. "Is that what you think?"

The truth was that I hadn't thought that, not until this minute. Not until he was throwing me out too. I couldn't speak, not with his grip. Instead, I made a half-hearted attempt to nod.

Reid walked me backward until I couldn't walk any farther. There was a wall or a door—I didn't know. All I knew was that I was caught between an immovable force of nature and an unmoving structure.

"Listen to me."

Did I have a choice?

"We can argue for the next fifty years over when we should have told Mason. I don't give a fuck. He was one of my best friends, so if you think I'm standing here without remorse, you're wrong. But not an ounce..." His voice rose. "Not one fucking ounce of that remorse has anything to do with us. You, Lorna Pierce, are not any of the things you said. For the record, I don't randomly screw. And a piece of meat?" His dark glare went from my head to my toes. "Sweetheart, you're barely a chicken nugget. But that doesn't stop the way I feel about you."

I found my voice. "You feel like you want me gone, just like everyone else."

"*Everyone* doesn't want you gone."

I took a deep breath, straightening my neck. "The only one who matters does."

"That's where you're wrong."

Before I could answer, his lips were on mine.

Strong, powerful, and possessive.

It was our first real kiss in a week. It was the first kiss that didn't offer sympathy. This kiss took unapologetically. The force bruised my lips as his tongue demanded entrance. This kiss was as far from sympathy as one could get. It was the blaze I'd seen in his eyes transformed into our connection. The fire blazing in his dark orbs had needed an outlet, and this kiss was it. Each punishing assault of his lips on mine was an out-of-control fire brimming with heat, passion, and desire.

My body lost rigidity as I melted toward him. This connection was an unmanageable wildfire ravaging everything in its path. A whimper turned to a moan. My arms moved up to his shoulders as the uncontainable heat filled me, twisting my insides, and dampening my core.

When Reid pulled away, he asked, "Do you know why you're wrong?"

Wrong?

I wasn't sure what he meant or was talking about. I couldn't think straight. "What?"

His strong body pressed against me, pushing me into the wall. Even through his blue jeans and mine, I could feel his hard and angry desire pressed against my belly. Along with all the passion, sadness and uncertainty wavered in the air, shimmering under the lights as his voice deepened. The tenor lowered. "I matter."

I tilted my head, trying to understand.

"You matter. My opinion, Lorna, it matters."

It was coming back. The reason I was leaving. "But...h-he said not to tell you."

"You didn't. I figured it out. I figured it out before I came up here. And before I came up here, I made one thing clear to Sparrow: for me to stay a part of this outfit, a part of our team, and a part of the Sparrow success, you are staying too."

A lump came to my throat as Reid's proclamation reverberated through me. "How? How did you figure it out?"

He shook his head once. "That's not what's important."

"But Mr. Sparrow?"

Reid didn't answer. Instead, in the common area of the apartments, he fell to one knee. "I never imagined doing this. I never thought I'd find someone who I loved so much that the idea of even a day without her would leave me helplessly empty." His cheeks rose as his lips curled. "So I don't have a prepared speech." He reached for my hands. "I don't even have a ring."

My breathing racked against my chest as my lungs fought for air and my eyes again filled with tears.

"If I could ask for your hand, I'd ask my friend. I'd tell him that I love his sister. I'd tell him that she's the first thing I think about when I wake and the last thought before I sleep."

My entire body trembled as impossibly more tears fell.

"I'd ask him to trust me with her because if he would, I'd do every damn thing in my power to make each day of her life better than the day before. I'd love and worship her. I'd take her hand." He squeezed mine. "And I'd walk beside her wherever life led us." He cleared his throat. "I would promise him that I was raised by two of the best women who ever walked this earth, and they taught me that women are God's gift to men. Women aren't meant to be ruled over, but made of Adam's rib to be a partner at our side. I'd promise him that I would do that. I would love you, stand beside you, lay down my life for you, and listen to you, because Gram always said that the only way to know someone is to listen."

He leaned over my hands and kissed my knuckles. When he looked up, I couldn't stop my smile. It wasn't diminished by the tears but enhanced.

"Lorna, I can't ask your brother for your hand, but I can ask you. Will you marry me?"

If I were to be honest, I had never imagined this scene either. I didn't have a speech in my head that needed to be said. There was a big part of me that wished Reid could ask Mason, that I could have his approval.

And then I did.

I looked over at the elevator doors.

Mason was there.

Not in reality, but spiritually, in my mind.

The glare was gone.

My brother was smiling at me—at us.

I wanted to ask Reid again about Mr. Sparrow. I wanted to know if he planned for us to stay here in this tower with them. And then I caught sight of the suitcases. In that second, I knew that I didn't care if we stayed or left. The only part that I cared about, the part that was deep inside me, was the desire to be anywhere with this man.

"Yes." I fell down to my knees so that we were eye to eye. "Yes, Reid, I want to marry you. I want to get to know you better. I want to fall asleep beside you and wake up with you." My smile grew. "I want to learn more about Gram, and I want to be the kind of woman she'd approve of for her grandson. I want to love you like you deserve. I know you couldn't ask Mace, but somewhere in my heart, I believe he would have said yes."

"Before or after he punched me?"

I smirked. "Probably after."

Reid pulled my hands upward as we both stood. "Earlier, what you said about not belonging here?"

I nodded as I looked at the suitcases and back to him. "I didn't. I don't know. He wants—"

"*He* is taken care of," Reid said resolutely. "The choice isn't his. It's yours. And you were right. You don't belong in Mason's apartment. You belong in ours."

Ours?

Nerves like small insects scattered through my bloodstream. I was prepared to leave alone. I was willing to leave with Reid—almost excited.

But to stay?

"I-I..."

Reid's smile bloomed again. "I know the decor is awful. I know it needs work to be a home. I guess to me it didn't need to be more than my space. That was before. I want it to be a home now—our home."

I looked around the common area. "But he owns this. And he doesn't want me here."

"He's changed his mind."

I shook my head. "I don't know him well, but he doesn't seem like the kind of man who often changes his mind."

"You're right again. He's not." Reid stood taller. "This time he did. I hope your choice is to stay because as of a few minutes ago, your airplane ticket was canceled. The money was retrieved from the account in Warwick. And the apartment lease will be cancelled tomorrow. As for the cash he gave you, do whatever you want with it."

My gaze narrowed. "You know about everything?"

"I told you. I figured it out."

"How?"

"Does it matter?"

Did it?

"You want to stay here?" I asked. "You and Mr. Sparrow are good? I didn't ruin it?"

More gently than before, Reid reached for my shoulders and grinned. "Lorna, the reason I know I love you is that question. Instead of worrying about the million things you could be worried about, you're asking me if my friendship with a man who tried to send you away is all right. I'm sure through the years to come, I'll find a thousand other reasons to love you, but right now, it's your amazing heart and your ability to care for people who may not deserve it."

"Does he?"

"Does who what?" Reid asked.

"Does Mr. Sparrow," I began, hesitant to ask, but needing to know. After all, my brother had befriended him, vowed to support him, and so had Reid, yet to me he was cold and indifferent at best. My question was genuine. "Does he deserve to have people to care about him?"

Reid nodded. "He does. He's complicated and driven. He feels guilty for what happened to Mason. One day, he'll be able to look at you and see you and not your brother. If it takes him a while, please be patient. Remember, we have fifty or more years. He'll come around."

"Are you sure?"

"I am."

"Then I trust you," I said, lifting to my tiptoes and placing a kiss on his cheek. I again saw the suitcases. "So you weren't throwing me out?"

"No, sweetheart, I was moving you in."

Opening the door to his, I mean *our* apartment, I grinned

at the one recliner and big screen television. "You're right. This place needs work."

"And you, the future Mrs. Murray, are the perfect person for the job." His eyebrows danced. "If you accept, I should warn you, there is a good chance that there could be inappropriate sexual advances on that job."

"As long as they're from you, I promise not to file a complaint."

LORNA

Present day

*M*y restless sleep was riddled with images, dreams, and nightmares. I continued on, disoriented, lost, and searching as I moved throughout alternate realities. The settings in which I roamed didn't stay the same, instead, changing like scenes in a poorly produced movie. At one moment the terrain was rough— hills to climb and obstacles to avoid—and difficult to maneuver. The world seemed without light—even seeing my hand before my face was a task. Trees and roots reached out, snagging my feet, arms, and clothes. I forged on, in search of what I wasn't certain, only that it was near. And then the foliage was gone, replaced by a stark, dried ground. In the sky, the sun shone unrelentingly bright, too bright, blindingly bright. Even my hands couldn't shield my eyes from the meltingly hot sun. My tired body became covered with perspiration, my mouth dried, and my exposed skin seared beneath the intense brilliance, and still I searched.

The dreams continued without end as I pushed myself beyond my own limits.

In my heart, I knew my goal was close, and yet I couldn't remember what it was.

I fought against the mounting resistance thrown my way, each step more grueling than the last, each movement of my arms more arduous. My breathing labored as the restraint became tighter and tighter. A scream boiled in my throat, stopped from escaping like the fizz unable to escape a corked bottle.

A stinging assault came to my cheek and then another.

I tried to lift my heavy eyelids.

The scene around me was out of focus.

Sound waves warped, their meaning lost to the odd bending.

I blinked against the brightness.

My eyelids fluttered.

Reality was returning.

I tried to shield my eyes, and then clear my eyes, to rub them, to remove the sleep accumulated in their corners.

I couldn't lift my arms.

Looking down, I blinked again, seeing the restraints binding my wrists.

One attempt to kick let me know my ankles were also bound.

My face moved quickly to the side as another blow came to my cheek.

The taste of copper filled my mouth.

I spat it away, red droplets spewing forward in the radiating light.

"Stop," a woman's voice said. It wasn't that she spoke the command with compassion. It simply was what it was.

I blinked again.

The illumination shone directly at me, making whatever was beyond difficult to see.

A man came into view, dark hair, a rigid clean-shaven jaw, nondescript eyes, and a towering presence. The mere fact he was not trying to hide his identity frightened me more than the menacing way he looked at me or the knowledge that he'd recently struck me. My instincts told me to look away to shield myself.

I didn't.

Defiantly, I lifted my chin as blood and saliva dripped from my gagged lips onto my shirt.

I looked from him to a woman who had stepped into my line of sight.

With blonde hair starkly pulled away from her face and slacks and a blouse that seemed out of place, it was clear this was the woman in charge. This was her show. Her frame may not have been large; her petite body and athletic build looked much like mine. Yet it wasn't her stature that illustrated her power; it was the venom displayed in her gaze and the determination in her expression. "It's about time you woke. I really am losing my patience with the likes of you."

The unflattering hairstyle wasn't what held my attention. It was the skin on the left side of her face. The surface appeared bumpy in a familiar way, reminding me of Mason's beneath his tattoos.

Prying my gaze away, I squinted my eyes and peered beyond the two individuals to the room around us. No longer were we in the cell I'd shared with Araneae. This room was different, unremarkable. The walls were the same cement-block motif. However, where the cell's walls were white, this room was gray with gray. We were within a gray box with a high ceiling.

Near the door was a large mirror, one that was most likely a one-way window. Set up a few feet away was a large light within a silver casing, shining my way. It hadn't been the sun I'd felt, but artificial light turned on high. The design of the room reminded me of an interrogation room on a television show or movie. There was even a small rectangular table with three chairs.

Only three.

I was in the fourth.

It was no longer placed at the table, but out into the room.

Uselessly, I pulled against my restraints.

As the woman walked closer, her shoes clipped on the hard surface floor. With a tug she pulled the gag from my lips.

For a brief moment I wondered if it was my blindfold from before. However, there were more pressing concerns.

As her nondescript gray eyes met mine, I bravely asked, "Where is my friend?"

She shook her head. "No longer your concern."

"Wait...what does that mean?"

The woman's voice grew softer, unnaturally sweetened and dripping with sickening syrup. Her head tilted in mock sympathy. "Your earlier display of concern was admirable."

I tried to remember. Araneae was brought back to our cell, but she wasn't speaking, wasn't moving. "She's my friend."

The woman's lips curled upward. "Aww. That's...sweet. Unfortunately, she wasn't mine." She shrugged. "And quite honestly, she was of no use to me."

"So what did you do? Where is she?" My questions came quicker. "Do you know who she is? Her husband would pay—"

The next sequence of events all happened quicker than I could predict.

The woman's nod to the man.

The man's slap to my face.

The force at which my head turned.

The tears, the blood.

They were a physical reaction to the pain, not emotional.

My tears for Araneae would wait.

My attention was on the here and now.

"Where is she?" I yelled.

"My patience," the woman began as she walked back and forth before me, "ran out on her." Her gaze came back to me.

"That doesn't leave much for you. While I'm not out to make enemies of her husband or yours, they're inconsequential and" —she shrugged— "I don't really give a damn."

This woman knew Sterling Sparrow's identity and regarded it as inconsequential?

"Who are you?" I asked.

"Your friend asked the same question. I had hoped you would be more original."

"Tell me she's all right."

The woman came closer and leaned down until we were eye to eye. "Is that all it would take, Lorna Pierce, for me to tell you? Would you believe me?" She stood with a grin.

Lorna Pierce, my maiden name.

My gaze went from the woman to the man. He was now standing behind her, his arms crossed over his chest in a silent demonstration of strength. I looked back at her.

"No," I replied. "I don't believe a damn word you say."

"You'd better hope I believe you, or you too will be deemed useless."

"Fine, new question," I said, sitting taller. "Who do you work for?"

"Aww, there we go. You are thinking beyond your friend."

I tried to concentrate on the here and now, not focusing on Araneae or where she could be. My energy was best spent not worrying about her baby or their future. Only for a moment, I imagined her back with Sparrow. I wanted that as much as I wanted to be back with Reid. I couldn't help that I loved my friends as if they were family. I did.

The possibility of Sparrow without Araneae was as painful as Reid without me.

We'd all worked too hard and too long to forge whatever it was we all shared. I wasn't willing to give up hope of us having it again.

The woman turned to the man.

I steeled myself, waiting for his abuse. Instead, he reached for one of the three chairs still at the table and carried it to the space before me. With the grace of a choreographed script, he turned off the bright light, leaving me with circles dancing in my vision. Then, he set the chair down and the woman stepped forward and took a seat.

It was as she sat that I noticed her left arm and hand. She was wearing a glove. It wasn't a medical glove as if to protect her from illness or germs that my bodily fluids could but didn't possess. The glove was white, much like gloves Michael Jackson or the Queen of England wore or maybe women in the mid-twentieth century with large hats as they went to church or perhaps the Kentucky Derby.

This wasn't Kentucky, to my knowledge, and we sure as hell weren't at church. I was fairly certain if we were on a spiritual precipice, this was the gateway to hell.

As the woman sat, she crossed her legs at her ankles. Her left hand gently fell to her lap. With her right unpocked— unscarred—hand, she tapped her chin. "Now, where to begin?"

I pulled at the restraints on my wrists, those binding me to the chair. "How about we start with untying me?"

She shook her head as her lips pursed. "No, that isn't where I was thinking." She tilted her head one way and the other, taking me in, searching my expression, perhaps my presence. "I know, Lorna. Start at the beginning."

My head bobbed as I tried to make sense of this. "Could I have some water?"

The woman's chin lifted abruptly.

The man behind her turned and stepped away. Opening the one door to the room, he left. In that brief second, I saw and heard nothing. There were no other people in the hallway. I couldn't even be sure if the walls were different than these. It was just more space.

Where are we?

It was then I recalled falling asleep with Araneae. "Was the water in the bottles drugged?"

"If I told you no...?" the woman asked.

I didn't answer. She was right again. I wasn't likely to believe anything this woman had to say.

I could ask if the bottle that I hoped was about to come to me was safe or I could refuse to drink it. Again, I wasn't certain I would believe anything these people said. I knew what I did believe: even without the earlier smoldering heat of the light, my thirst was growing by the moment, as was, unbelievably, my hunger.

I had no way of knowing how much time had passed since our last meal.

How was I moved from the cell to this room without my knowledge?

It reminded me of a baby, one that fell asleep at Grandma's only to awaken at home. Yet I didn't have the sense of trust and safety that was innate in a baby. Thirty-five years had whittled that away, leaving a select few as those who deserved my blind allegiance.

How long had it been since Araneae and I were taken?

How long since I'd seen Reid?

The questions flowed.

Instead of thinking about them or contemplating their answers and how they fit into the future as I'd know it, I stared at my captor.

This wasn't like the books I'd read. Although I'd at one time considered myself *Cinderella,* I wasn't Belle in a grown-up version of *Beauty and the Beast.* There was no redemption or future love story to be written in this current scenario. This wasn't a fictional trope. This was the dangerous reality of the life I'd accepted, and my captor was an evil woman with judging eyes.

When she didn't respond again, I asked, "What do you want to know? What beginning?"

REID

"I had to get out of the house," I said into the microphone as the Montana landscape was laid out below us like a green and brown blanket, interrupted by blue streams and rivers and surrounded by deep purple mountains and white snow-capped peaks.

"I can use your help." Mason's voice came through the earphones though he was sitting beside me in the pilot's seat. This plane had two seats, pilot and copilot. There was a jump seat in the back, but not one of us could or would want to fit.

"Sparrow came up with me this morning," Mason continued, "and we made a few observations. My opinion is skewed so I decided to get yours."

I could have given my opinion as I usually did, from behind a screen or two or five. I could have pulled up the real-time satellite images I'd successfully hacked. And while under normal circumstances that was sufficient, being here in Mason's plane high above the ground, I understood the deficiencies in my *normal*. The satellite imagery paled in comparison to the reality of flying a little over five thousand feet in the air.

"When's the last time you flew in something this small—an airplane, not a helicopter," Mason asked.

I shook my head as I looked at the array of gauges, levers, and switches on the control panel before us. "I don't remember," I answered honestly. "If you want me to take the controls, I hope you have parachutes."

Mason scoffed as we banked toward the west.

"Helicopters and the Sparrow fleet," I went on, "are my main modes of air travel."

"I miss piloting," he said. "Small planes were always my thing. Sparrow and Patrick had an affinity for helicopters. I didn't care for the restriction. While I wouldn't take this baby out in a lightning storm, it's more predictable in wind than a chopper."

His statement made me think. "How was the weather Thursday?"

Mason turned; his gaze came to me as he grinned. "See how getting up here helps?" He inhaled and looked out the front windshield. "Clears your mind."

It had been two days since the women were taken. In the last forty-eight hours we'd made headway. We knew the kidnappers arrived via helicopter. It wasn't as large as Mason had feared, based on the landing skid length. I had been able to utilize cameras on Mason's land to determine that the chopper came from the west and also returned west. With the help of satellite as well as survey maps from the state of Montana, we located possible hideouts. The capos who arrived from Chicago were mobile and checking out all large and small leads.

While progress had been made, no contact had been attempted to negotiate their release.

With each passing minute, hour, day, my nerves were stretched to their limits. I wasn't alone. I knew that. The man flying the plane beside me was also rightfully on edge.

After a few more minutes, Mason hit a button on the side of his headset. As he did, my headset went completely silent. Such as the effect of noise-canceling headphones, there was nothing—a soundless void. When I looked at my brother-in-law, he removed his headphones and placed them on his lap.

Following his lead, I did the same.

Immediately, sound was back, no longer a hum but a roar. The engine and spinning propeller keeping us airborne rumbled with vigor, making the use of headphones seem obvious. I wasn't one who rode a motorcycle, but it could be equated to the same phenomenon. Imagine the rush of air as a motorcycle cruises at sixty to seventy miles an hour. Imagine no helmet, the wind whisking past your ears, and the person in front of you speaks.

That was the impression as Mason yelled above the roars. "I'm going to contact the Order."

I knew why he'd brought me up here. It was the one place, without the headphones, where we could speak in complete privacy. "I thought you'd cut all ties."

"I did. But that doesn't mean I don't have means." He weighed his words. "Before those ties were severed, we figured out Top's identity."

My jaw clenched as the scenery below lost its luster. "The last time you tried to contact the Order," I yelled at the man less than three feet away, "you had all of us backing you up."

"The last time was for *my* freedom. This time it's for Lorna's and Arnaeae's. Do you think Sparrow can keep a cool head if he would suspect we're dealing with his wife's captor?"

I wanted to believe this wasn't the Sovereign Order, the organization that Mason had been involved in while he'd been away from us. However, if we were dealing with a warring outfit—a cartel, bratva, or Cosa Nostra—we would have heard something. The guilty party would claim responsibility and seek to make a profit on their bounty.

Patrick and Sparrow had been in contact with various outfits throughout the country, more accurately, throughout North America. If any organization had the queen of Chicago or the wife of one of Sparrow's trusted advisors in their hold, it would make sense that the organization would do its best to capitalize upon it. They would brag about their capture, ask for obscene amounts of cash or merchandise, or offer to trade the women to another organization to pay back a deal gone wrong.

Instead, for over forty-eight hours there has been silence.

Instead of answering Mason's question about Sparrow's ability to keep a cool head, I shook mine. "Sparrow wants a target."

That was the truth in a nutshell.

Not having anyone to direct our anger toward was almost worse than having a target. If we knew anything at all, we could plot and plan. Uncertainty continued to mount with each passing minute, hour, and day. Not knowing who we were fighting against left the Sparrows in a suspended state of flux.

"If I'm right," Mason said loudly, "Sparrow will have a fucking huge target."

I wished we were on a motorcycle. I'd tell him to pull over and let us converse in private without screaming. "What do you plan to do?"

"I have to go to Washington DC" —the last known location of the man known as Top— "if that's where Top still is. I did a search last night. Congress is out for summer recess. Edison Walters—Top—has a residence in the city. I found no record of his travel." Mason shrugged. "That doesn't mean anything. I'm sure he's capable of incognito. If he's physically out of DC and with the Order, I'll need to make an SOS call. I'm hoping I don't have to go that far."

"You want to show up at his house?"

"The deal I made, the one for my freedom, was with him.

He has that kind of power. If the Order decided to go back on that deal, he would know and by all rights, so should I be informed, not that the Order usually informs its targets."

"And when you show up, if that deal was rescinded without your knowledge, what will he do?" I asked. "Kill you on sight. Part of your agreement was to forget the Order and everything associated with them."

"Well, they didn't give me the fucking drug, so the memories are there. For the last two years I've kept them buried, but who the fuck else would take my sister and be after my wife?"

We were all certain that Laurel had been the target. It was the little bit of the puzzle that made sense. I let Mason's words sink in as I thought about the Sovereign Order.

It was difficult, if not impossible, to describe the power of the Sovereign Order in a few words, paragraphs, or even in numerous lengthy biographical tomes. For lack of a better description, the Order was a government-funded agency outside of the three known branches of government. It didn't exist in the executive, legislative, or judicial branch. As far as elected officials were concerned, not one knew of its existence.

Patrick was our expert with money. Give him a trail, let him follow a lead, and he'll see patterns others miss. He determined that the agency was funded by the US government through pork-barrel expenditures enacted by the legislative branch and signed off by the executive branch.

One or two sentences in a thousand-page bill would

appropriate funding for what appeared as a benign beneficiary. Perhaps it was a philanthropic organization or perhaps it was an organization centered on the arts—whatever was hot at the time. One hundred thousand here. A million there. Over the years the amount of needed funding has increased as the operational costs increased.

The reality was that in a trillion-dollar bill, a million was easily overlooked. If that million was further divided into smaller sums and the beneficiaries were not connectable, the Sovereign Order remained properly funded for generations.

This wasn't a new process.

It didn't begin with the current administration or the one before that. It wasn't secured by funding proposals from one party or even always one of the two most commonly known. The clandestine organization succeeded beneath the radar because it did not hold any affiliation to man, woman, or party. It held no loyalty other than to that of the republic. The Sovereign Order existed to maintain a balance of power, to right perceived wrongs, and to do so without the scrutiny associated with our governing bodies.

International terrorists were assassinated. Domestic threats were eliminated—at the Order's discretion.

The press reported the consequences without true knowledge of the actions.

Sometimes erroneous sources claimed responsibility. The Order didn't barter for the spotlight.

Rarely were reports accurate.

All in all, the Order operated by the old adage: the end justified the means.

The way my brother-in-law became a part of the Sovereign Order was another of the Order's less-than-transparent modes of operation. The government agency that doesn't exist was primarily manned by soldiers who also no longer existed.

It was the perfect combination.

The Order saved Mason Pierce from death, not to return him to his life, but to give him life anew as a dead soldier walking. After all, what do dead soldiers with no memory of their life have to lose?

The answer was nothing.

Most soldiers in the Order's army do not walk away. Again, how does one walk away from an agency that doesn't exist? As had been and continues to be my brother-in-law's modus operandi, he was the exception to rules and the forces of nature that by definition couldn't be denied.

Mason's death that Sparrow witnessed wasn't his death but his rebirth into the Sovereign Order.

However, unlike others who had been like him, Mason's unwavering blind allegiance to a covert organization was now severed.

He'd come back to his real life, agreeing to leave the knowledge that was supposed to be known by no living person, in his past.

The question now was, Did that past come back to claim him?

"I'm going with you," I said, looking Mason in the eye.

When he didn't respond, I did. "You didn't bring me up here to clear my head. You brought me up here to tell me your plan. And you fucking knew how I would respond."

"What if something happens here?" he asked.

"Patrick and Sparrow will be here. I wouldn't let you do this alone last time; I'm sure as fuck not doing it now if it means Lorna's life."

Mason nodded. "We need to come up with a plan. All four of us can't fly off to DC."

As he spoke, he banked the small plane, turning back toward the direction of his ranch.

Afternoon sunlight shimmered like a reflective gleam off of something on the floor of the canyon below.

"Did you see that?" I asked.

"What?"

I lifted my headphones back to my head and nodded toward Mason. Soon we were again communicating without screaming. "Can you bank back around? It's probably nothing, but I swear that I saw something."

The plane began to move as I'd asked, yet Mason's reply was less positive. "We've been over this canyon before. It's not far from my property line and isn't even fenced. Out here is just wild land. Hell, locals could set up a campsite and it would take Seth a solid fortnight before he knew."

I saw it again. A glistening coming from the canyon floor below. If Mason were right and locals had camped, it could be something as simple as discarded tin foil. "Can you land?"

Mason surveyed the land below. "Not without beating the shit out of the landing gear."

"Can you go lower?"

A few minutes later we did a third pass and according to the gauge, our altitude was dangerously low at just over a thousand feet. I searched the area where I'd thought I'd seen the reflection. "Fuck, Mason. There's something or someone there."

LORNA

"*B*eginning..." I began. "I was born in Chicago, Illinois."

The woman's lips curled upward. "You were born at South Shore Hospital. Your mother tested positive for cocaine upon your birth so you were released to the custody of your grandmother, Margaret Pierce."

I sat back and let out a long breath. "Well, you asked for the beginning. I don't know any beginning before my birth, and it seems you're well informed."

"Who is your father?"

"I don't know."

"Who fathered your siblings?"

Siblings?

She knew about Mason and Missy?

"I don't know," I repeated.

"Did you ever hear a name?"

I scoffed. "I heard lots of names while growing up. I would suppose you could give me any name, Tom, Steve, John...and I'd say I heard it. My mother was a fan of men."

She nodded. "I'm not surprised you're a bit more worldly. Your friend wasn't. Despite her odd string of homes, she was...sheltered. That's not you, Lorna, is it?"

"What do you want from me?"

"Tell me about your grandmother."

My grandmother's face flashed before me, the gentleness in her gray eyes, and the love in her touch. I focused instead on the woman before me. "I have nothing to say about her."

"Was she abusive?"

"What the hell is your problem?" Yes, I realized I was hardly in the position to argue, but at the same time, I wanted to know this woman's endgame.

"I'm going to assume your question is rhetorical?"

"No, she wasn't abusive. My grandmother was a wonderful woman. My grandfather, Clinton Pierce, was also a good man who worked hard. He died of natural causes when I was very young. My grandmother raised...me" —I wasn't bringing my siblings into this— "until she died."

"Hmm." The woman leaned forward. "Now, tell me about Laurel Carlson."

"Laurel...she is my sister-in-law. She's who you wanted. That first day, those men asked if we were Mason's wife."

"Very good. Why were you at her home?"

"She's my sister-in-law as you know." If this lady knew the

hospital where I was born, I could assume her knowledge was more widespread. "We were visiting."

"Do you like her?"

Her question took me aback. I had liked Laurel when we were children and her father counseled at the local Boys and Girls Club. I'd liked her when she went off to college and when I'd mailed her the news of Mason's demise. And then when she showed up in the tower, I remember being shocked. Of course, I was even more shocked when I learned of her companion, my brother. As I watched the two of them together and I saw what she'd done to return Mason to not only me, but to himself, my affection grew from like to more. I grew to love her.

I looked my captor in the eye. "I can't recall ever not liking Laurel Carlson."

The woman scoffed as she leaned back in the chair and tapped the fingernails of her right hand on the armrest. Her nose scrunched. "Really? She's not a bit too goody-goody for your liking?"

"No."

"Her *Little Mary Sunshine* attitude doesn't get annoying to you?"

Instead of answering, I sat straighter. "How do you know Laurel?"

"So you're admitting she possesses the qualities I stated?"

"No. I'm admitting that you seem to be speaking from your own experience. That isn't how I see Laurel at all."

The woman's head cocked to the side. "Come on, Lorna.

Who are you?" Before I could answer, she went on, "You're no one, nobody. You were born in a hospital that provides indigent care. Your own mother was too strung out to want you or pay for your birth. Until you met your husband, you made a living cleaning other people's shit—literally. You worked in a cheap hotel. Before that, you waited tables. In high school, while Laurel was in physics club and Latin club, you were working weekend nights at an all-night diner to have money for food. I don't mean lunch money. It was more than food. You were paying for a room in someone else's house because no one besides you gave a shit if you lived or died."

I worked to keep my emotions at bay. I wanted to tell her she was wrong. Mason cared. He'd left for the military, but he was sending me money. I just was too stubborn to spend it.

Before I could, she continued, "And your *fr-ie-nd*" —she elongated the word— "the one that you were so caring toward, what was she doing? Oh, she was at an overpriced private school in the mountains of Colorado."

I didn't have an answer for this woman. Nothing she said was untrue, yet that wasn't how it was with Laurel or Araneae. I'd never felt like a no one when I was with them. I never looked at their upbringing as making them better than me, only different. We all had different backgrounds. The men did too. It made our family eclectic and strong. Our bonds were formed over less superficial things than high school activities.

I forced a smile. "I'm sure," I began, "it's the lack of nutrients, or maybe the drugs you keep feeding me, but I'm missing your point. I don't hate Laurel or Araneae. One is my sister-in-law and friend, the other is my friend."

"Which one?"

"Which one, what?"

The woman sighed as she shook her head. "You figured it out, I want Laurel. You and Araneae were taken by mistake. Which friend do you believe deserves to be saved? The sun is setting on one of them." Her smile grew. "And as their mutual friend, I'm asking for your advice."

I tried to make sense of this. "So, Araneae is safe?"

"She could be."

"Her baby?" I asked as the door opened and the man from before entered.

He was carrying a tray that looked like one that would be delivered to a hospital room. There was a water bottle and a decanter that could possibly contain coffee. Even just seeing it made my body cry out for caffeine—my temples throbbed and dark spots danced across my vision. A little over a year ago I'd tried to decrease the amount of caffeine in the tower. That didn't last long. My intentions were good, but even I was in withdrawal. I've heard I could have pushed through.

I didn't.

There was also a covered dish.

I wasn't sure what it contained or how it would taste, but its mere presence had my stomach grumbling with hunger pains.

The woman stood and nodded to the man. He moved her chair to the table and set it before the tray. She walked toward me. "I tell you what. I'll give you some time to think—not that she has much." She lifted her chin toward the dark-haired man. "After I leave, Jet will untie you." She shrugged. "You can eat or not eat. Your choice. But while you're spending your time, think about which friend should be saved, which one deserves another day. Hurry, before it's too late for Araneae."

I looked up at her. "Why are you doing this?"

"Besides the obvious?"

My head tilted.

"Because I can."

"Why do you want Laurel?"

Her nose scrunched again. "I could tell you, but then you'd know too much. If you choose wisely, maybe your days are without a near end." She turned and nodded to Jet before she started walking toward the door. At the last moment she turned. "There's nothing—no drugs—in the food or water. I have no reason to drug you at this moment. Of course, you don't have to believe me." With that she turned and left the room.

I closed my eyes as Jet came nearer. I listened to his boots on the floor and inhaled as he came closer. There was a tug at my ankle. When I opened my eyes, he was holding a large knife and slicing through what appeared to be duct tape holding me to the chair.

"Who do you work for?" I asked softly.

His light brown eyes peered my way and then he silently went back to his work. I had no reason to assume this man would tell me anything or even be kind. After all he was the one who had awakened me to his slaps. Nonetheless, I was limited on options.

"If you help me escape, I can pay you more than you make from her or whoever she works for. I can protect you too."

He didn't respond, but his chin lifted ever so slightly.

The woman may have been out of the room, but Jet's minimal movement reminded me of the large one-way mirror I'd forgotten about. She was gone, but she was connected.

"The offer stands," I whispered even more quietly.

"Don't move until I leave," he said as he stood, folded the blade back into the knife's handle, and pushed it down into the pocket of his blue jeans.

I gripped the armrests, willing myself to stay put.

Once he was gone, I assessed the door. It didn't make the multitude of clicks that the door on the cell had made.

Did that mean it wasn't locked?

What would I find on the other side?

Well, one possibility was Jet with his six-inch blade.

I waited another thirty seconds before I stood. My muscles ached as I took a step and then another. I flexed my fingers and arms, celebrating my small slice of freedom.

The first thing I reached for once I made it to the table was the bottle of water. Such as the ones in the cell, the seal clicked. I couldn't be sure if the contents were safe; however, I knew that without the water, I wouldn't last. The human body needed water to survive. Food was secondary, but lifting the cover on the plate, I knew I would eat whatever was there. This time it was what appeared to be too-orange macaroni and cheese, a slice of ham, and a pile of soft, overcooked green beans.

"Boxed macaroni and cheese," I said, thinking of Araneae. She'd joked about cooking that for Sparrow a long time ago.

New tears saturated my cheeks and stung my newest lacerations as I sat and forced myself to eat and drink. There wasn't any cream or sugar for the coffee. I wanted to speak to the window and tell my captor that if she'd really done her homework, she'd know I liked cream.

That thought didn't last long.

"Which one?"

Which friend should live?

That wasn't a question I could even consider.

REID

Nine years ago

*M*y pulse echoed in my ears as I entered Lorna's and my apartment. The day was here and I was stereotypically anxious. I wasn't nervous. This was the right decision, the right next step, just plain right. That didn't ease my fretfulness.

For a moment, I stood in the front entry and stared into the living room and dining area of the kitchen. The sight before me calmed my thoughts. In the month's time since Lorna had moved in, she'd made both obvious and subtle changes that together transformed this from my space to our home. I'd encouraged her every step of the way, prompting her to check out various shops and retailers. With the war we were currently fighting, I asked her to do as much online and over the phone as possible.

She said the floor-to-ceiling windows and the fireplace should be the focal points, not the television. It was an interesting concept I was willing to explore, as long as the television stayed.

Throughout all her virtual explorations, Lorna spoke about color in a way that brought a smile to her face. It was something that Mason had told her as a child. I couldn't recall the exact wording, but in essence, color gave her strength, security, and serenity. That was why I was surprised when our new sofas were delivered and capos brought them up to the apartment.

They were gray, sleek, and minimalist.

It was the next box that brought the radiant smile to her face.

Throw pillows in various bright colors.

Oranges.

Yellows.

Blues.

Reds.

There was an array of shapes as well as shades.

Lorna's next addition was a dining room table. After all there was a light fixture on a chain. It made sense to put a table below it. I'd always eaten at the breakfast bar. We still did occasionally, but we now had options. Next, a centerpiece and placemats arrived; like the pillows, there were so many colors.

There were many more spaces around the apartment that I was excited to have her decorate. Seeing Lorna's vibrant personality come out in her choice of decor filled me with satisfaction like I'd never felt with this apartment in the past.

I looked at my watch as I sat the large box I'd brought on the new sofa. It was nearly eight in the morning, the morning of our wedding.

I supposed if I'd given my wedding much thought, I'd imagined one day having a ceremony in a church, the pews filled with family. Part of me feared that Lorna had imagined the same thing. With the way our life was, that wasn't an option.

The day we planned was less festive—yet the outcome would be the same.

Last week we'd gone with the protection of Sparrows and applied for our marriage license. A small fee was all it took. Today, with the same bodyguards, the two of us will make our trip to the Cook County Marriage and Civil Union Court.

Retrieving the long white box, I made my way to our bedroom and pushed open the door. This room was still as it had been the first time I'd snuck my fiancée into my bed. It would take time to make the entire apartment ours. What we'd done in this room to make our future ours didn't include decor. It was the time we'd spent as one, the hours spent holding her as she contemplated love and loss, and the nights we'd talked until the sun rose.

I laid the box down on the unmade bed as I walked toward the attached bathroom. The door was slightly ajar, but my steps stuttered, wondering if this was a good time for me to interrupt. As I came to a stop on the threshold, the door opened, pulling inward as Lorna looked up at me.

Wrapped in a fluffy towel, the dew of a recent shower upon her alabaster skin, as water dripped over her shoulders and her red tresses hung in damp curls, she was the absolutely most beautiful woman I'd ever seen. A smile came to my lips as I reached for her left hand. The ring I hadn't had when I proposed glistened in the bathroom light. With a simple platinum band and a six-point setting, the two-carat diamond was similar to my future wife, not overdone but simply stunning.

I lifted her hand to my lips and brushed a kiss over her knuckles. "I hope you haven't changed your mind."

Her lips curled upward and her green eyes shone. "About what?"

Unable to keep my hands to myself, I reached for her waist and lifted her to the vanity. Working my way closer still, I moved between her knees as she leaned back upon the counter. It was the perfect view, seeing her front before me and her back in the reflection. Taking the edge of the towel in my grip, I gently eased the hem away and let the towel fall.

"Reid," she said, her gaze fixed on me. "Isn't this bad luck, seeing a bride on her wedding day?"

I took a step back to better see.

I scanned her freshly showered body, now completely bare. From her freshly painted toenails to her wet hair, Lorna was spectacular in an uncomplicated way. She didn't need makeup or expensive dresses. Her smile could light up a room, her voice a song, and her touch was like that of a master artist bringing not only vibrant color but also a settling hue.

"Is it bad luck to fuck the bride-to-be?" I lifted my eyebrows. "I mean, it's my last chance to make love to Lorna Pierce."

She sat forward, her knees still spread, and reached for my neck, pulling me toward her. "I don't know. Are you going to fuck me or make love?"

With her question, my circulation rerouted. "Lorna, I didn't come back here for that." She peppered my neck with kisses as she untucked my shirt and began to pull it over my head. "I-I came to give you something."

Lorna leaned back, her fingers roaming my abs, her firm round breasts and tight pink nipples on display. "Then give it to me. I don't care. Fuck me. Make love to me. I need to know you're here. I want to feel you inside me. I want to know that's where you belong. And I belong with you."

"Fuck." The word rumbled off the tile and chrome like thunder before a storm.

Leaving the towel behind, I slid my arms around her, one behind her back and the other under her knees. She was light as a feather as I carried her back to the bedroom and laid her upon the bed.

"What's that?" she asked, seeing the box.

"It can wait."

A wide smile broke across her face as I reached for my belt. Within seconds, I was dressed the same as she. In other words, we were equally undressed. Lorna lay back, lifting her arms as I climbed slowly up her body. Inch by inch, I kissed and nipped her ankles, knees, and thighs, until I found my way to her core. The wetness from her shower was mostly gone, but as my tongue delved between her folds, new wetness was found.

Her hips bucked as I took my time, sucking and teasing. With one hand I held her in place as her legs tied me in a vise. Her moans and whimpers filled our bedroom. It was right as she was on the edge, as I felt her legs grow stiff, that I moved higher. Leaving her warm, wet pussy, I found each of her perfect breasts. They were barely a handful and perfect. I could worship them for hours. The way her nipples tightened and areolas darkened was like a jolt to my dick.

Lorna's receptiveness was a drug to my libido. I wanted to see how far I could take her, to what new height. It was as if each time we were together, I needed to see if I could elicit more, because more for her was also more for me.

"Reid."

My name echoed off the walls.

A deep kiss of her lips and I found my place. Centered at her entrance, I watched her gorgeous face as I pushed my way deeper. The way her back arched, her neck stretched, and her lips opened to the perfect "o" kept me going. Her body quivered as I sank deeper. Her pussy contracted, tightening, yet her essence bid my entry.

"I'll never get tired of how fucking good it feels to be inside you."

Green eyes peered up at me, shimmering in the morning light coming from our open curtains. "Good, because I'm loving the way it feels to have you there."

"I want to make love."

Her smile grew. "I think that's what this is."

I lifted my chest above her, my arms on both sides of her beautiful face. "No, Lorna. Tonight, when we're Mr. and Mrs. Murray, I plan to fuck you. All night. But right now, I want to make love to you. I want you to know how fucking much I adore you, how much I know this is right. You and me. We're right."

Lorna wiggled beneath me, making me unbelievably harder. "Make love to me. And tonight, I'll be ready."

I did.

Time passed without notice.

Our bodies covered with perspiration as the temperature between us grew. It wasn't an explosion, but a simmering inferno, the slow and steady flame that provides life. If I could ask for anything it would be that the comfort we shared, the pleasure we both gave and received, that those qualities would never fade, that on our fiftieth anniversary we would feel the way we did right now.

Over and over Lorna found ecstasy and more than once I did too. We were different in many ways and yet we fit together like I'd never known. Perhaps it was the contrast, the sheer beauty in my dark skin against her light, my girth to her petite frame, or my deep, guttural growls to her soft mewing, that made our union feel so right.

Or maybe it was as I'd said—we were simply meant to be.

In the entire universe, we were meant for one another. The stars aligned the night we met. There was no other explanation and no course of action but for us to stay as one.

It was true we'd both experienced life's ups and down. Lorna wasn't my first and I wasn't hers. That didn't matter. What mattered was that we would be each other's last. For the rest of our lives, for eternity to come, we were meant to be with one another.

Straddling me, Lorna's back arched again as she came undone. With a satisfied sigh, she collapsed upon my chest, our bodies still linked.

"I hear your heart," she said, her cheek against my chest.

"What is it saying?"

"It's saying if we plan to make it to our appointment at the court, we need to get dressed."

I lifted my arm to see my watch. "Shit. The car is coming in less than an hour."

REID

Nine years ago

"Shit," I said again before lifting her face, her cheeks flush from our activity. "Sweetheart, have you eaten?"

Her gaze glistened. "Not food."

She eased off of me. "I need to shower again."

"Shit." The word seemed to be foremost in my vocabulary. "The car will be here."

Lorna sat up on the bed beside me and looked down at the floor. "Are you going to tell me what that is?"

"Oh." I hurried off the bed and lifted the box, straightening its lid and the bow. "It's something for you."

She peered my way suspiciously. "Reid, we said no wedding gifts."

"It's not a gift."

Her chin came up as she giggled. It was a beautiful sound. One I wanted to hear over and over. "I think it was the big bow that might have thrown me off."

I pushed it closer. "Okay, it's a gift. But it's not a wedding gift."

"I see. It's a gift on our wedding day...but not a—"

"Jesus, woman, will you just open it?"

Her smile sparkled as she loosened the bow. It didn't seem to matter that we were both still completely naked or that we'd recently completed a marathon lovemaking session. We were two people completely comfortable in one another's presence.

When she lifted the lid, her gaze came to me. "It's a big box."

"I've heard size is important."

Lorna's eyes scanned me up and down. As she made her way up to my eyes, she said, "Not as important as skill. But when you have both, it's the best combination." She looked back into the large box and pulled away the tissue paper. "Oh, Reid."

When she looked up, her green eyes were glassy.

"It's not supposed to make you cry."

Lorna reached in and pulled the ivory dress from the box. It was satin, and designed to fit only her. I'd found her measurements from the time Mason had arranged a special dress for her, the night we'd met.

"I hope it fits. I know this isn't a real wedding, not with a church or any of that, but I wanted you to...well, I guess, I thought..."

Lorna climbed to her knees and scooted to the edge of the bed until she was right in front of me. She lifted her arms to my shoulders. "It is a real wedding. We're getting married. And this is beautiful. I was debating on what I even had to wear with my grandmother's necklace. I figured it wasn't important, not with everything that is happening and has happened."

Palming her cheeks, I gave her a kiss. "You are always the most important. I know me and I know my work. If I ever forget that, I want you to remind me."

Lorna nodded. "I will." She crawled off the bed. "Now go. I have no time to get ready."

"In a few hours it will be official." I reached for her hand and took one last look at all of her. "You will be mine, forever."

"Well, unless you want me to go to the court nude, you better let me get ready."

I walked to the closet and grabbed my suit from a hanger and my shoes from the rack. "I'll get ready in one of the other bedrooms. I'm making you a sandwich."

"And a cup of coffee," she called as she hurried back into the bathroom.

Half an hour later, I paced by the breakfast bar where a turkey sandwich and cup of coffee waited. Every few seconds, I turned toward the hallway, wishing for Lorna's entrance. Every other second, I checked the clock.

I sent another text to the capo whom I'd chosen to drive us.

We had another four canvassing the courthouse waiting for our arrival.

Things were still hot with a few of the remaining old Sparrow guard. And then there were the issues with the McFadden outfit. I wasn't taking a chance for anything to ruin my wedding day.

My phone buzzed with a text message.

"NEED YOU ON 1."

"What the fuck?"

The text message was from Sparrow.

Instead of texting back, I hit the call button. I didn't wait for him to say hello. "I'm not available."

"Fuck that," he said. "Sparrow comes first. McFadden just pulled some shit, and we need you down here. I need you to access their communication."

Communication?

"Fine," I said, trying to keep my voice low. "It can wait until we get back. Our appointment is in forty minutes. The car is waiting."

"No, the car isn't. You're needed here. Come down to 1 and bring Lorna." The phone went dead.

I continued to stare at my phone, expecting something —anything.

Heat rose under my collar as my heart beat in double time. This was beyond what I expected from even Sparrow. My jaw clenched. There was nothing that couldn't wait. "Fuck him."

I began to text our ride when I heard footsteps coming from the hallway.

I looked up as my breath caught in my chest.

Standing at the end of the hallway was a goddess.

I began at the top of her head. Her red curls were pulled up into a twist with small curls near her cheeks. In her hair was a hairpiece made of tiny ivory satin flowers that had been with the dress. She wore more makeup than normal, but not too much. Her eyes were striking and her lips pink. Around her neck was a simple string of pearls. They were her grandmother's and she'd said she would wear them. The dress I'd chosen fit like a glove, the neckline showed just a hint of the round breasts I knew were there. It accentuated her trim waist, and flowed in what the saleswoman called a straight skirt that landed asymmetrically near her calves. Whatever, she was dazzling.

On her feet were matching ivory shoes, the kind that showed the tips of her toes.

When I looked back up, she was staring my way. "So?"

I laid my phone on the counter. "You're beautiful." It was woefully insufficient, yet it was simply the truth. No, it went further. She wasn't just beautiful. She was the most beautiful bride anywhere since the dawn of time.

Lorna stretched her neck as she scanned me and my suit. It was the one I'd worn the night we met except I'd exchanged the tie for an ivory one, to match her. "You're very handsome yourself." She looked past me. "Who were you talking to?"

I forced a smile. "No one. Come on, our car is waiting."

It had better fucking be waiting.

When we entered the elevator, I hit G for garage. The doors closed and the elevator moved, stopping too soon, on floor 1. Floor 1 was the Sparrow floor where others were allowed. Capos came there to make reports. Deliveries were made there. It was secure, but not as secure as 2 or the apartments or penthouse.

I knew that it was possible to redirect the elevator. I just thought it wouldn't happen to me.

"What's happening?" Lorna asked.

I took a deep breath. "Nothing. This will just take a minute."

When the doors opened, Patrick was waiting. He looked as he always did, wearing a gray suit. That meant nothing. If he wasn't in pajamas, he wore a suit. The man didn't understand casual wear.

I didn't speak to him. I sent my message in the form of daggers flying from my dark gaze.

"It will only take a minute," Patrick said apologetically.

"I'll wait with Lorna." He turned his eyes on her. "You look beautiful."

"Thank you. Um, I'm sorry you couldn't come. I guess Mr. Sparrow doesn't want too many of you in one place."

I let out a breath. "Where the fuck is he?"

"Conference room four," Patrick said as he continued his conversation with Lorna.

I turned on my heels, a million thoughts racing through my mind. The first was my resignation. I believed in everything Sparrow stood for, but I wouldn't, I *couldn't* allow him to undermine the one part of my life he couldn't control. If Sparrow couldn't handle that separation, then I couldn't handle our connection.

I reached for the door handle on conference room four, not thinking about its size. It was where large meetings were held. We had conference rooms of all sizes. Four was the largest. As the door opened, I stopped.

I wasn't an emotional man. One didn't do what we did, live through what we'd done, and wear emotions on his sleeve. But at this moment, words failed me as the room blurred.

Quickly, I blinked away the moisture as I took in the room.

The conference table was gone. Chairs lined both sides in sets of two. There weren't a lot present, but the ones that were there were filled. I recognized faces. There was Dr. Renita Dixon and her husband. Jana and her husband, Keaton and his husband, and Marianne and her partner were present. Apart from the doctor, they were our crew on most flights and their significant others. There were also others present who were considered trusted in the Sparrow organization.

At the front of the room, along with flowers and candles, was Sparrow, dressed as he did for Michigan Avenue. He wore a dark suit and tie.

I made my way to the front of the room. "I was about ready to tell you to shove—"

Sparrow stopped my word with a sad smile and a shake of his head. "I don't give a fuck how you want to be married. But *his* sister deserves better than some sorry-ass courtroom." He turned to the man at his side. "Reid Murray, this is Judge Bronson."

I'd never met Judge Edward Bronson, but I was aware of him and his affiliation to Sparrow. He was a federal judge, a bit above performing weddings. Instead of saying that, I offered my hand. "Thank you, Your Honor."

"I'm assuming you have your license?"

I tapped my suit coat. "I do. We filed last week."

"That's all we need."

Someone near the door hit a switch and killed half the lights. The change made the candles in the front glow as music came from some unknown source. The guests stood.

And then the door opened.

I took a deep breath as Lorna came forward, escorted by my friend Patrick.

In her grasp was a bouquet of flowers. Unlike her dress, it was made up of an array of brightly colored flowers. I hadn't thought of a bouquet. I didn't know if it was Sparrow or Patrick, but whoever chose the arrangement, chose perfectly.

When Lorna came to a stop before me, the rest of the room faded.

I took her hands in mine as she passed her bouquet to Patrick. Granted, in his gray suit, he didn't look the part of a maid of honor. Then again, in the Sparrow world, nothing looked exactly as it appeared, even the man to my side. Sparrow had self-appointed himself my best man, and as long as I didn't give it too much thought, it too was exactly what was needed.

Less like a civil wedding and more like the one Lorna may have imagined, the Honorable Judge Bronson began. He talked of love and commitment. He asked for rings.

We had those.

And then he asked, "Do you, Reid Murray, take Lorna Pierce as your wedded wife? Do you promise to love, honor, and keep her only unto yourself for as long as you both shall live?"

Lost in her stunning green stare, I found the right words. "I do."

He then asked her a similar question. I listened for her answer.

"I do."

REID

Present day

I called the coordinates of the object we'd seen to Patrick on the plane's two-way radio. It didn't take long to realize that it would be a two-hour trip by motorized vehicle. Mountains and valleys had a way of slowing down ground travel.

"I have to land," Mason said. "I'll take us lower. Look for a clearing."

"Why do I suddenly wish you had a thing for helicopters?"

Mason nodded. "It would be a hell of a lot easier to land."

"We'll leave right away," Patrick said through the headset.

"Wait," I offered. "We're going to land. It could be a false alarm."

"Over there," Mason said, pointing to the north. "I can

land there. We'll have to walk back to whatever it is we're seeing."

I nodded his direction. This very well could be nothing. I knew that, but after over forty-eight hours of nothing, I was desperate for something. Flying back to the ranch and leaving the discovery to Patrick and Sparrow, who were at least two hours away, didn't bode well. Too many things could happen in two hours. If this was simply trash that was reflecting, it could blow away. But if it was a person, he or she would be susceptible to the intense afternoon sun, scavenger birds, or poisonous reptiles. I pushed through, refusing to give those scenarios more thought.

Mason's knuckles blanched as he steadied the control column. This controlled the pitch of the plane—nose up or down—and the roll—left or right bank. His neck straightened as his legs extended, pressuring the rudder pedals controlling the steering and the right-left movement.

As the plane banked and Mason lined up the settings with the ground below, I reached for the strap over the door. I knew that it wouldn't hold me if we crashed. It was purely my need to hold on to something. My only other alternative was to hold on to the copilot's control column. We both knew that wasn't a good option.

The plane slowed as Mason adjusted the rudder and wing flaps. We both swayed from side to side as he worked to steady the fuselage. On this model of aircraft, the landing gear didn't retract, so it was down and ready.

Lower we went.

This canyon was situated in a north-south corridor.

The plane wavered, shifting us one way and the other.

"Crosswinds," he muttered under his breath as he worked to keep us steady.

My breath held in my chest as the ground came closer below us until we made contact.

Our bodies bounced within our safety harnesses as the wheels touched the ground. The uneven terrain made the plane jump and spring as we slowed. The brakes upon the landing gear squealed and the wing flaps quivered loudly as rocks and gravel peppered the undercarriage. Finally, we came to a stop.

I released my breath.

Hitting levers and switches, Mason quickly unbuckled his harness. "I need to check for damage."

"Will you be able to take off from here?"

His green eyes came my way. "I sure as fuck hope so. If not, I'll need an oversized flatbed to get this plane back to the ranch."

I inhaled, conscious of the odors around us. There was a warm scent associated with the rubbing of the brakes and the tires skidding upon the hard-packed ground. What I didn't smell was fuel or smoke.

Good signs.

Mason was out of the plane, walking quickly around the fuselage and inspecting the landing gear, the underside, and the wings. By the time I joined him, he'd made a full circle.

"What do you think?" I asked.

He looked at me with a grin. "I think I'm a fucking better pilot than I gave myself credit for."

I scoffed. "Okay, pilot extraordinaire, I'm calling Patrick."

Pulling my phone from my pocket, I hit his contact and placed my phone to my ear.

I waited.

Nothing.

Bringing the screen before me, I saw the symbol in the corner.

"Fuck," I mumbled. "No signal."

Mason looked up and around. "We're too low. The mountains are blocking the cell signal."

Nodding, I went back to the plane and turned back on the two-way radio. Using it would take away from the much-needed battery power, essential for starting the plane and working the controls during takeoff. As I turned on the plane, I noticed the fuel gauge—a little over a quarter tank. That was plenty to get us back to the ranch.

Would it be enough for takeoff and returning?

I spoke into the microphone, "Charlie Omega Alpha calling home base."

"Home base." It was Sparrow's voice. "Tell me what's happening."

"We landed." I looked around. "We're in a valley within the canyon at the far west of Mason's property. We don't have a cell signal."

"What did you see?" he asked.

"I don't know." I admitted. "Fuck, it could be nothing. It'll take us some time to get to the coordinates. If there's a signal there, we'll call. If not, we'll report back as soon as we get back to the plane."

"There are capos about forty-five minutes out. I've sent them to the coordinates you sent."

A sigh resonated from my chest. "I fucking hope this isn't a wild goose chase, Sparrow."

"It's the most we've had. Call as soon as you can."

"We will. Out."

I flipped the switches, cutting all power to the plane. When I backed out of the copilot's seat, Mason was there.

"Ready?" he asked.

"You have a first-aid kit?"

He nodded. "Yeah." He walked around to a cargo hold and opened the door. When he handed it my way, he asked, "Wishful thinking?"

"Like Sparrow said, it's the most we've had." I looked off to the south, covering my eyes from the afternoon sun. "This way." When I looked back, Mason had water jugs. "Wishful thinking?"

"Thought maybe it might be a good idea not to pass out from dehydration before we report back."

"Good plan." I turned to the south. "This way."

The ground under our boots was hard and packed. The grass was brown and brittle. The dry season was about ready to give way to the rains of autumn. In another month, where we landed and were walking could be a stream or raging river.

Above us the sky was blue with white clouds floating here and there. In the distance, the taller mountains glistened with their white snowcaps. We both pushed on, through the crunchy grass, up and down hills. The shine I'd seen before was nowhere to be found. Mason and I exchanged glances. Each passing minute and football-field length we traveled lowered our expectations.

"Maybe I imagined it," I said, stopping to take a drink of water and wiping the sweat from my brow.

"We're here," he said, looking at his phone. "The coordinates connected to satellites, not cell towers. Let's spread out and cover this area. The grass is tall in some spots." He lifted his eyes to the horizon. "We need to be certain that we don't miss anything before we turn around."

I walked to our left while Mason went to the right. The plan was to go one thousand yards and then loop back toward one another. With each step, I scanned the ground in all directions. The dry grass and hard-packed earth were all fading together.

My feet stilled and hearing strained.

I waited.

Had I heard something?

It could have been an animal scampering to shelter from the hot sun or a bird searching for food. I looked up, scanning the sky.

The sound came again.

"Mason," I called. "Come over here."

"Did you find something?" he asked as he turned to come my way.

Once he was near, I lifted my hand. "Hold still and listen. I swear I heard something."

The breeze that had tried to upend the plane whistled in our ears as we both slowly turned complete circles. The topography of the canyon caused sounds to echo. Maybe I was hearing my own breaths, my own steps on the hard ground, or simply the wind.

Nerves tingled my skin. Every receptor was on full alert.

"P-lease."

Mason and I froze, our eyes speaking volumes.

He spoke first, calling to the wilderness, "Is someone there?"

Nothing.

"Hello? We're here to help you," I called louder than Mason.

"H-help."

We both began to run toward a clump of large rocks. This time of day, the far side was a small amount of shade in the vast sunshine. Mason and I both came to a dead stop as we saw her.

"Holy shit," I mumbled as I went closer. "Araneae."

It wasn't a question. I knew her identity.

Despite the sunburned skin, matted hair, bleeding feet, and tattered clothes, there was no doubt of her identity. We'd found Araneae Sparrow.

I knelt down beside her and lifted her head as Mason handed me the water. "Araneae," I spoke softly.

Her swollen eyelids fluttered as soft brown orbs came in and out of sight.

I scanned her prone body searching for injuries while confirming her baby bump. Other than the obvious dishevelment, she appeared unhurt. "Araneae, can you drink?"

Her head bobbed as her dry, cracked lips parted.

I inclined the bottle, bringing the liquid to her lips. After a few seconds of her swallowing, I pulled it away. "I don't want you to get sick."

Her eyes blinked, each time staying open longer and focusing on me. "Help..." Her hand went to her throat. Her large diamond wedding band and engagement ring shone, reflecting the sunlight like a beacon in the wilderness.

I reached for her hand and turned it ever so slightly.

That was it. That was the flash I'd seen.

It was a miracle that her ring could make a flash strong enough for me to see, but there wasn't another feasible answer.

"P-please..." Her voice cracked.

I returned the bottle to her lips. "Drink a little more. It's okay, don't force talking."

She nodded as she again swallowed the clean, clear liquid. After I pulled it away, she said, "Thank you. Um..." She turned from me to Mason and back. "C-can you please help me?"

"Where is Lorna?" I couldn't stop the question from spewing forward.

Araneae looked down. "Please, I'm pregnant."

Mason nodded and began to walk away. With his phone in the air, I knew he was trying to get a signal.

I turned back to Araneae. "Are you okay?" I asked. "Your baby?"

"I think," she said as moisture came to her eyes. Her nose flared as a renegade tear scurried down her dirty, sunburnt cheek. "I think I should see a doctor."

"We'll get you to one." I let out a long breath. "Please, what do you know about Lorna?"

Her head shook. "I-I..."

It was going to be all right. We had Araneae. I had to believe we'd have Lorna too, soon. I lifted my head and looked in every direction. "Is she here?"

"I don't know," Araneae said softly. "I'm not sure where we are."

I laid her head onto the ground before taking her hands. "It's going to be okay, Araneae. Can you stand?"

Her eyes focused on me as she tilted her head. "My name is Kennedy. Do I know you?"

LORNA

I held tight to the metal frame of the bunk bed, waiting. The door closed and locks engaged. A moment later, light illuminated the cell I now occupied alone. Heaviness filled my chest and questions packed my mind and heart with concern as I ripped the blindfold from my eyes and took in the room I'd once shared.

What had happened to Araneae?

My thoughts went back over the recent past.

After the question-and-answer session, I was fed. It wasn't more than an inexpensive insta-meal. The macaroni and cheese was gritty with its instant cheese powder. The ham was processed, reminding me of a canned meat we'd eaten as children. The green beans were overcooked and came from a can. It was surprisingly delicious, all in all. I was unsure how long it had been since I'd eaten and as I lifted each forkful to my lips, my stomach rumbled with satisfaction. In that moment, I didn't care if I was fed filet mignon or instant macaroni. It was food.

The old proverb, beggars can't be choosers seemed appropriate.

However, I hadn't begged.

If the food had been withheld much longer, all bets were off.

After the food was gone, I paced the interrogation room, waiting and expecting the woman in charge to return for my answer. It caused the nutrients to percolate in my stomach. Finally, the door opened. It wasn't her but Jet.

With my blindfold back in place, I was made to walk back to the cell.

Considering I'd arrived to that room unconscious and drugged, I preferred the new option, even if I was expected to do it without sight.

Throughout the journey, Jet was my escort. Since I'd seen him in the lighted room, I assumed the blindfold was to keep me from seeing the other parts of this...whatever this was. We walked for longer than I expected, going up and down concrete stairs. I had no way of knowing if it was necessary or a ruse to make me believe this compound was larger than it was.

At one point, we stepped through a doorway. The floor beneath my bare feet changed to sharp gravel. There was just enough space under my blindfold for me to see the ground below. Even though it was nighttime, the outside was artificially illuminated. Once outside, I lifted my covered eyes to the warm breeze.

While the breeze whistled through the air, there were no sounds of night creatures as I would hear on trips in rural Illinois. No crickets or frogs. I listened for birds or bats. I imagined fireflies sparkling over a field. Yet I had no indication that any of those were present. The only distinguishing characteristic was a scent of pine. I had visions of Sparrow's cabin or maybe the air fresheners shaped like pine trees.

The gravel bit into my feet, yet Jet didn't slow.

As we moved through the night, there were no other voices. No hushed conversations. No sense we were being watched.

How many people were here?

Also absent were the sounds of motorized vehicles, engines revving, tires on asphalt, or horns honking, all common things to hear in Chicago. As we walked, the gravel continued both ahead and beside me. There wasn't enough of a gap in my blindfold to see beyond it.

Was there grass?

Was there sand?

I didn't know.

And then we stepped up and over a new threshold, entering a building—a different one or the same. I didn't know. The air inside was noticeably stuffier as if the day's heat had settled within the cement-block walls, humidity dampening the concrete floor to where it wasn't wet, but it wasn't dry. The scent of pine was replaced by the musty odor I knew in our cell. This building contained more doorways and stairs. We stopped and locks clicked. We moved forward and doors closed behind us. I didn't know if we walked in circles, up the same steps we'd gone down, or repeated various hallways.

Finally, I was shoved through a doorway.

The room was dark.

Even blindfolded, I knew this was the same cell as before.

I felt it under my skin.

There was a familiarity that welcomed and saddened me.

I instinctively stepped toward the bunk bed, held onto the metal, and waited.

The door closed, the locks engaged, and the lights came on.

If it was possible to feel a multitude of emotions at once, in that split second, I did.

There was hope that when I removed my blindfold, Araneae would be present, fear for where she was and what was happening to her, and wishes that she was safe and back with Sparrow.

The reality was much lonelier.

Taking off my blindfold, I confirmed my fear: the room was without another prisoner.

That's where I was now, back where I'd been with Araneae.

This cell contained a toilet and sink, two amenities missing from the interrogation room. I took care of business, washed my hands and face, and made my way to the bottom bunk. It was as we'd left it. The pillow and blanket from above were on the bottom bunk. I lifted the blanket to my face and inhaled, subtle scents reminding me of my friend. I imagined the way she'd been, and as tears filled my eyes, I reminded God of the deal we'd made.

"Please keep her safe. Please keep their baby safe. I willingly offer children I might one day have had."

Thinking about babies, I admitted to myself that I was honestly inexperienced in their care.

Ruby had joined us as almost an adult.

As a child, I cared for my younger sister, but she'd been only a year and a half younger than me. When she was an infant, I was a baby. We grew up together, yet somehow, I'd taken on the role of caregiver along with our grandmother. We'd all taken our places in the life we'd been dealt. Mason was the provider. At only a little over a year older than me, he'd watched our grandparents. When they could no longer provide, he stepped into a role he was much too young to occupy.

The woman's statements were the catalyst for my thoughts.

She'd said I was nothing, no one.

Perhaps to some people it could appear so. Those weren't people who mattered.

Even during those difficult times, I never felt as though I was no one. I was Lorna Pierce. I was a sister, granddaughter, daughter, and a girl, turned teenager, turned woman. I was a friend and a wife.

The woman had been scarily accurate in my biography. My jobs had been menial.

That didn't make them less.

I worked hard.

I never expected anyone to hand me success. Even when Mason would send me money from the service, I saved, not spending more than necessary. When he brought me to the tower, I refused to be a freeloader. The men had their work that kept them busy for hours late into the night and early into the morning. The tasks I took on weren't earthshaking.

I cooked.

I cleaned.

I did my best to make the tower a home for all of us.

Memories filled my head from years ago.

And then there was the missing piece of her interrogation.

My husband, Reid Murray.

Did she know about him?

How could she not?

Yet she referred to me as Pierce not Murray.

My husband had never made me feel like a no one.

From the night we first met, he treated me with love, respect, and sincerity. In the midst of some of the darkest times, he held my hand and lifted me up. My mind went to the other men in the tower—Mason, Sparrow, and Patrick.

I thought about the other things the woman had said, about Laurel and Araneae.

How could I dislike them for their upbringing?

Wouldn't that be the same as if they disliked me for mine?

We all came from different backgrounds. That's what made us stronger not weaker.

I may not have the degrees Laurel had, the business savvy Araneae had, or the ingenuity Madeline had, but I realized, sitting on the bunk by myself, that I had something that the awful woman didn't have. I had friends. I had a family made out of love and respect. I would not give that up. I would not offer one of my friends as a sacrifice.

What the hell did she think this was?

It wasn't *Sophie's Choice*.

I peered around the room.

Clearly, I was at a disadvantage, but at that moment, I didn't care.

I wouldn't give up either of them.

Wrapping the blanket from the top bunk around me, I laid my head on the pillow and closed my eyes. I'd dream of safety and believe that Araneae was safe and that my safety was about to transpire.

There was no way to judge time. It was difficult enough while sleeping. Add no windows, no change in lighting, and no sense of day or night and the task was impossible.

Maybe ten minutes passed. Perhaps it was four hours or six. I didn't know.

I woke with a start, sitting up near the wall, and pulling my knees to my chest. I'd slept long enough to fill my bladder. That could wait as the door was opening.

"Good morning, Lorna," the woman said. Jet was at her heels, his arms crossed over his chest. "Time is up. I need your answer."

LORNA

Nine years ago

*W*ith a blanket over my legs, I lay in the corner of our new sofa surrounded by colorful pillows as I read an out-of-print book I'd recently found at a secondhand shop, *My Life as it Didn't Appear*. I'd been curious about it since I'd met the subject at a debutante party in New York. While I'd attended the party as a favor to Mason, that night proved pivotal in changing the course of my life.

Reading this book, I realized other people's lives can turn on a dime too. It was hard to imagine that the beautiful woman I'd met was the same person who described being kidnapped by a wealthy man and taken to his home.

A knock on the door of our apartment pulled me from my reverie. A quick check of the clock told me that it was nearly nine at night. I had no idea of the particulars involved, but as soon as Reid and I finished dinner, he hurried back to 2. It was the floor between the apartments and 1, where our wedding took place.

It was where Reid spent an abundance of his time.

Laying the blanket on the sofa, I peered down at my blue jeans and shirt. I wasn't dressed for company, but there were few options in this tower. I expected to open the door to find Patrick. It was my experience that Mr. Sparrow chose not to frequent this floor.

The knock came again.

"Coming," I called as I hurried toward the door.

My breath caught and my neck straightened as I opened the door to be met by dark eyes and a foreboding expression. I'd been wrong. This wasn't Patrick. With the exception of my wedding day, Sparrow had done his best to avoid speaking to me. "Mr. Sparrow? Reid isn't here."

"I know that. I found this in the kitchen of the penthouse," he said, holding an envelope forward.

It was one I recognized right away. It was the one I'd found on Mason's kitchen counter, the one filled with United States and British currency.

"Yes, sir, I wasn't sure how to give it back to you."

Sparrow took a step back into the common area and ran his free hand through his hair. When he looked back, his eyes were darker than before, filled with emotions I wasn't certain I would—if I could—identify. From the way his body tensed, I didn't think he wanted to acknowledge them either.

"We need to...we should talk."

I held tightly to the door with one hand and the jamb with the other. Loosening my grip, I took a small step backward. "You're welcome to come in." When he didn't answer, I added, "It's your place."

"No, Lorna, it's Reid's...and yours. Don't ever confuse that again."

Unsure how to respond, I nodded.

"Come upstairs." He turned toward the elevators.

My feet remained planted to the floor beneath them. When he looked back, I struggled for a response.

"Lorna."

"Mr. Sparrow, maybe when Reid gets back here? Or I could call him."

He let out a long sigh and came back toward me. "I'm not your enemy."

I was back between the door and jamb. It wasn't as reassuring as my brother on one side and my husband on the other, but it was all I had. "No, sir. You're not and I know that. I meant what I said before; thank you for the wedding. It was more than I could have imagined."

"I'm not good at some things," he said.

It was a small bit of humility, more than I'd ever heard or seen from him in the past. Sterling Sparrow was always in control, always the one with the answers. He didn't apologize because in his eyes he was always right. This admission might have seemed insignificant to others, but not to me. In this short time, I recognized it for the monumental statement it was.

"I'd like to talk to you in my office upstairs. Can you do that?" He waited and finally added. "Please."

I looked down at my sock-covered feet and when I looked up, I nodded. "Yes, I can. If you don't mind, I'll put on some shoes and be right up."

Without another word, he nodded and headed toward the elevator.

Closing the door, with my nerves already in tatters, I contemplated what he wanted to say. Resigned to my commitment to follow him, I hurried toward our bedroom closet in search of footwear. As I slipped my feet into a pair of flats, I decided whatever it was that he wanted to say, I could rule out another attempt to persuade me to leave, but then again, I couldn't be sure of anything.

When I stepped back into the common area, the envelope he'd held was lying on one of the sofas. My name was still on the outside as it had been when I first saw it. Shaking my head, I picked it up and stuffed it in the back pocket of my blue jeans.

I pushed the button for the elevator and waited, too nervous to give the near future too much thought. I could text Reid and tell him where I was going, where I'd been invited, but somehow that felt like a violation of whatever trust Mr. Sparrow had bestowed to me. If Mr. Sparrow had wanted Reid with me, he wouldn't have come to the apartment when he knew Reid was gone.

Once inside the elevator, I pushed the P. It was the button that would take me to Mr. Sparrow's penthouse. While the apartment floor had been divided into three apartments for Mason, Patrick, and Reid, there were two floors above that made up the penthouse. In the few months I'd been here, I jokingly referred to it to Reid as Sparrow's castle in the sky.

The entire penthouse was sleek and lavish with modern yet rich decor. The feel was light and open, not ostentatious as it could be, but elegant yet comfortable. His decorator must have convinced him that the floor-to-ceiling windows were the correct focal point. Everything was top of the line, from the appliances in the kitchen, to the fixtures throughout and the artwork upon the walls. While I'd seen most of the first floor, I had never entered his private office. I did, however, know where it was located.

The elevator stopped and the doors opened to a hallway. I stepped out onto the marble floor and looked both directions. If I went to the left, the hallway would take me to the front of the apartment, the location of the main entry that no one used. It would also take me to the large staircase leading to the second floor. If I continued on, I'd find a large kitchen, sitting rooms, a dining room, and more.

Taking a breath, I turned right. Despite the elegant sconces upon the walls that illuminated my path with warm golden light, my skin chilled. The small hairs on my arms stood to attention, and my steps slowed as I approached the partially closed door.

Taking a deep breath, I lifted my hand to knock. Before I could, I was bid entrance.

"Come in, Lorna."

I pushed the tall door aside and stepped inside.

Like most of the tower, Mr. Sparrow's office had the stunning floor-to-ceiling windows. Despite the darkening sky and twinkling lights beyond the large panes, they didn't capture my attention, not as much as the man who had invited me here.

Mr. Sparrow was seated behind a large wooden desk with ornate carvings. Compared to the rest of the apartment's furnishings, including the others in this office, it seemed ostentatious and out of place.

The desk did, not the man behind it.

Mr. Sparrow tipped his chin toward the two plushy upholstered accent chairs opposite the desk. "Have a seat."

Before sitting, I removed the envelope with the currencies and placed it on his desk. When he didn't speak, I did as he asked, sitting near the edge of one of the chairs. I couldn't pinpoint the reason for my posture. Maybe I was poised and ready to run back to the floor below.

Truly, with the way my heart thumped erratically in my chest, I wasn't certain of my next move.

After I was seated, he spoke, "That money is yours. It was given to you."

I gripped the chair's arms, bracing myself to respond. "Thank you. I believe it was given in expectation of my departure. I didn't leave. Therefore, the money isn't mine."

Sparrow leaned forward, placing his elbows on the desk before him. His jaw clenched as he stared my direction. Moments passed. His fingers intertwined until they loosened, and his arms folded one over the other on the desk's surface. I imagined the ticking of a clock. Maybe it wasn't my imagination. Hell, there could be a clock, a grandfather clock or a mantel clock. I wasn't sure, and I was too nervous to peer about. Finally, he spoke, "That expectation has been replaced by others."

"The expectation for me to leave?" I asked, clarifying.

Sparrow pushed back his chair and stood in one fluid move. He took a few steps as he spoke, "Lorna, since your arrival, I have been busy. There were and are more things happening than I could possibly articulate. Due to those preoccupations, I believe I have been" —he stopped walking and looked directly at me— "aloof."

My lips came together, wondering if I should agree or suggest more descriptive adjectives.

He asked, "What do you know about me?"

LORNA

Nine years ago

*M*r. Sparrow's question lingered in the air as I searched for words, knowing that my brother's name was no longer welcome in conversation while simultaneously wondering how honest Mr. Sparrow expected me to be. "I know you met...*everyone* while in the army." I chose the word as a way to include my brother.

Sparrow nodded.

"I know that you're the heir to Sparrow Enterprises."

He nodded again.

"I know that after your father died, your mission as well as the others' has been to seamlessly take over his dealings."

Mr. Sparrow gripped the back of his chair. "And you learned all of this from...?"

I shrugged. "Everyone." I thought about that. "Not so much Patrick. And *everyone* never gave me specifics. I was given enough pieces that I put it together. Am I wrong?"

Sparrow stepped away from the desk and walked toward the windows. "Your assessment isn't inaccurate." He turned back toward me. "I had everything planned."

My mouth grew dry.

"Nothing" —he looked around the room and out to the city— "...was left to chance. I'm a very particular planner down to the minutest detail."

"Except for me," I said. "I wasn't planned."

His dark eyes met mine. "Not entirely. You weren't in my plans. The thing is, if I try to think back, you were planned by him. He'd never hidden the fact he had a sister whom he cared about. Out of all of us, he was the one with a real connection. I didn't try to understand—or take the time to consider—that his love and concern would affect me in any way."

I swallowed the emotions he was evoking.

"When he brought you here, I told myself it was temporary."

I began to stand. "Mr. Sparrow—"

He lifted his hand, stopping me. He waited.

With an exhale, I resumed my seat.

"The plan I made for you in England," he said, "wasn't done in haste or out of malice. It wasn't a bad offer."

My head shook. "No, it wasn't."

His gaze went to the envelope on his desk before

returning to me. "You're here now, and I have wrestled with how we can make it work."

"You don't want me to leave?" I asked.

"This isn't about wanting or not wanting. You aren't leaving."

"But you—"

"Lorna," he interrupted, "even if I could forget that you're his sister, I can't forget that you're now Reid's wife. My detailed plans of the future involve your husband. I'm sure you know that he is a genius when it comes to all things technological. His ability is unmatched, not only in what he knows, but what he's able to learn in a short time. I saw it when we fought for our country. I watched him under duress. I saw his honor and commitment. I was fortunate enough to be considered his friend. Through that time, I knew without a doubt that Reid would be an invaluable asset to my plans. I don't want to consider the need to replace his skills."

Replace Reid?

"He doesn't—I don't believe he wants—to be replaced."

Sparrow's chin came up and the hint of a smile came to his lips. "That's nice to hear. He told me something different."

I stood. "He said he wants to leave you and the Sparrow organization?"

"No," Mr. Sparrow clarified. "He said he would leave if you did."

I thought for a moment. "That makes me, what, the consolation prize?"

"No, Lorna. This isn't about what you are. It's about my

eyes opening and accepting that sometimes plans change. I don't fucking welcome change, but that doesn't matter. It doesn't stop it from happening. My choice is to accept it or risk greater loss. My role in...all of this...is to lead. If I can't accept that my friend found a person he loves, it makes me a shitty leader. If that's the case, everyone should leave."

There was something about Reid telling Mr. Sparrow he loved me that made me smile. "I love him too, every day more than the last. I suppose it could look like I'm an opportunist—"

"Because you chose a life of danger, a life of secrets, and a life that will include isolation? What part of that was an opportunity for you?" He lifted his arm toward the window. "You were given a golden ticket to get the fuck away from here and" —he looked back at me— "you didn't choose the freedom of a new life. Hell, you chose love. That doesn't make you an opportunist, Lorna, perhaps a martyr."

"No, Mr. Sparrow. Being with Reid isn't a hardship."

Sparrow nodded and looked down at a chess set sitting on a round table between two chairs similar to the one I'd been sitting in. When he looked up, his gaze was again dark and clouded with emotions. "This chess set is never to be moved."

"Okay."

"I trust very few people."

I nodded.

"I don't know you well enough to make an informed decision. I trust Patrick and Reid with my life and have. I also trusted your brother. He trusted me, and I let him down."

I wanted to interject, to tell Mr. Sparrow that he hadn't let Mason down, but I couldn't make the words form as Sparrow continued speaking.

"The thing is, by trusting them it means I should trust their intuition. You had and have their trust. The most vulnerable a man can be is in sleep, and for the last few months, you've been beside Reid in his slumber. That's the kind of trust that isn't earned easily." He walked back to his desk chair and spun it toward him. "I can't ask you to trust me. You don't know me, not really. And what you do know or should know is that I let your brother down in the most grievous way."

"Why do you want me to trust you?"

He let out a long breath. "Because this...this tower was constructed to house the people who mean the most to me and to Sparrow. I will spare you the details, but when it comes to creating a home-like environment, I'm at a complete loss. Before" —he feigned a grin— "when we all moved in here, we were finding our way in both the takeover and in our assigned space.

"I've seen the change in Reid. I've seen a man who can work twenty-four seven suddenly care about dinner and getting back to his—not mine but *his*—home. I've listened to a man who could say ten words in a day give me an oration about what matters most. I don't want your presence to divide us. I need those two men on my side every hour of every day. I will work diligently to make my dreams a reality, and in the process, not let either of them down while helping to fulfill their goals.

"I asked you here tonight knowing that for that goal to be achieved, we need to work as a unit. One. Not three or four entities."

"And how can I...?"

"You were doing it, before we lost him. You were helping. I'm not asking you to work for me. You aren't an employee, any more than Reid or Patrick. I'm asking that even though you married Reid, maybe you could do some of what you were doing before for all of us."

"You mean like cooking and cleaning?"

"This isn't meant as a menial request."

"I-I—"

"It is the opposite," Mr. Sparrow said. "I didn't understand it before, but now I do." He walked back to the chessboard. "I never investigated hiring someone or a service to clean the different apartments because as I said, it's a matter of trust. I know there are others who would do it, people who would willingly do that out of a false sense of gratitude or others for the money. I don't truly know most of those people. I don't want a stranger in my home or yours."

"I wasn't sure that you wanted me up here," I admitted.

"I do, if you are willing. Just don't move the chess pieces."

A smile came to my face, raising my cheeks and curling my lips. "I promise."

"I'll have Reid set you up with an account to buy any household necessities. There isn't a checks and balances,

Lorna. I don't need a spreadsheet. Once my trust is given, it's without question until the day I regret that decision. I don't want to regret this decision."

Suddenly, what he was asking of me seemed even more important. "You won't, sir."

"What I would like more than anything is to not think about it, but to know it is taken care of by someone I trust."

"So, you're asking me to be kind of like the house manager."

Mr. Sparrow grinned. "You can be in charge of your title. I'm not a big fan of titles, especially amongst friends. Sterling or Sparrow works for me. No more mister or sir. Can we agree to that?"

"I think so."

"Besides the chessboard, my only other request is that you only enter the second floor of the penthouse when I'm away."

"I can do that."

Sparrow let out a long breath. His grin appeared more genuine, bringing light to his dark gaze. "I bet you didn't count on getting three men when you agreed to marry Reid."

I shook my head. "I don't know for sure what I anticipated. I probably didn't count on his friends being more than his."

"Well, you have that friendship too. I should warn you. Friendship doesn't mean I won't be a pain in the ass sometimes."

"Noted," I said with a smirk. "I heard that about you too."

"I'm sure you did."

"This will be new to us and you. Work it out. You're the house manager or whatever you want to call yourself. The schedule is yours, the spending account is yours. There is only one steadfast, unbreakable rule that goes along with this arrangement."

"What is that?" I asked.

"Believe us."

I took a breath. "Okay."

"Lorna, I mentioned that by staying here, you chose danger over freedom. I let your brother down because for a moment in time—one that I would fucking take back if I could—in that moment, I forgot to fully appreciate the true risk that goes with our world. One time I underestimated the consequences. He brought you here to keep you safe. Keeping you here does the opposite. You're now the wife of a top Sparrow. You're a target to others. If we tell you that you need to stay in the tower, believe us.

"It's because as God is my witness, I will never underestimate that danger again. It isn't because you're a woman, a sister, or a wife. It's because Patrick was right. You're family. We protect what is ours."

"Reid gave me a similar warning after his proposal."

Sparrow grinned. "It's a good thing it wasn't before. You might have changed your answer."

"I don't think I would have."

"Do we have a deal?"

"Yes." I started to say *Mr.* Sparrow but stopped. "Yes, Sparrow, we do."

He motioned between us. "This doesn't need to be mentioned again."

My eyes opened wide. "What doesn't?"

He nodded. "Very good." His smile faded. "Or him. My thoughts about him are known. I don't need nor have time to relive them."

It was the same warning I'd been given by Reid, not to mention Mason's name in Mr. Sparrow's presence. "I'm sorry that I remind you of him," I said earnestly.

"Fuck that. Be your own person. *You* are now an intricate part of us because of *you*. Reid loves *you*. Patrick picked out flowers for *you*. I asked *you* to come up here. *You* did." He continued to emphasize the personal pronoun. "He will always be a part, but he isn't your part. No one is but you. Thank you for coming up and talking to me."

Tears prickled the backs of my eyes as I grinned. "Thank you for asking me." I turned to leave.

"Lorna?"

I spun back to him and his desk. "Yeah?"

"Your breakfasts were nice."

My smile grew. "Tomorrow at seven."

"This floor," he said.

"This floor."

REID

Present day

The small plane approached the landing strip at the main house. Although Mason's plane only contained the pilot and copilot seats, in the aft there was a third jump seat. While neither of us would have easily fit, Araneae did. Throughout the flight, I continued to check on her, offering her water and asking if she was all right. Since she didn't have headphones, it was more of a labored game of charades.

Before heading away from where Araneae was discovered, Mason and I did a scan of the area, determined to not leave Lorna behind. Both of our searches came up empty. While I didn't want to think about my wife alone on the canyon floor,

I also couldn't delay getting Araneae a.k.a. Kennedy back to the house.

As soon as we reached the plane, we radioed the house. Sparrow assured us that they'd be waiting along with medical help including the doctor who checked out Madeline and Laurel after the attack.

"No one is close," Mason said to me after the radio conversation, speaking of the doctor.

"Sparrow will have a fucking helicopter fly the doctor to the ranch. I have no doubt."

Mason's green stare, the one like his sister's came my direction. "Lorna is still alive."

His response wasn't in regard to what I'd said, but to what I needed to hear. I inhaled, letting his words sink in, taking them as gospel, and refusing to believe otherwise.

Once the plane came a little closer to the main house, my prediction came to fruition. A helicopter sat near the outbuildings in the area where the kidnappers had landed. The markings on the tail indicated it was from a level-three trauma center in Butte.

"You were right," Mason said, before peering back over his shoulder and back. His green gaze questioned along with his one word. "Kennedy?"

"Yeah, it was her name...before..." I didn't finish. It all happened before Mason's return; however, the story wasn't secret.

"Before Sparrow?"

"You know the story," I said. "It's complicated."

"She didn't know me, which is understandable," Mason said softly into the headphones. "Seems like she would have known you." When I didn't reply, he added, "Surely, she'll know Sparrow."

"I fucking hope so."

As we touched down Sparrow, Patrick, Madeline, and Laurel stepped out of the hangar. Sparrow barely waited for the plane to stop when he took off running toward us. As Mason turned off the controls, I unbuckled myself and opened the door to reach the jump seat.

"Are we to the hospital?" Kennedy asked.

"No." I looked at her harness and back up to her light brown eyes. "May I help you?"

"Yes," she answered quickly with a nod. "If we're not at a hospital, where are we?"

Mason had taken off his earphones. "This is my ranch, mine and my wife's. The hospital is farther away. Your husband had the trauma helicopter brought here."

Her eyes opened wide. "My husband?"

Mason's gaze went to mine.

Before we could comment, Sparrow was there, reaching for her hand as she began to stand. That didn't last long before he had her in his arms. "Tell me you're all right," he demanded.

Araneae blinked as she took in the man holding her. New tears glistened in her eyes. "Sterling?" She laid her head against his as her body trembled with gut-wrenching sobs. "Sterling. Oh...Sterling."

His dark gaze looked our way. There were words of gratitude he couldn't convey. Instead, he said, "I'm taking her to the house. The doctor is waiting."

We both nodded.

Once he was gone, I turned to Mason. "What the fuck?"

His head shook. "I don't know." He looked toward the others. "Hey, Doc?" He wasn't calling to the doctor who had come at Sparrow's bid, but to his wife, Laurel.

We began walking toward the others as they came toward us.

"How is she?" Laurel asked.

"What about Lorna?" Madeline asked.

We both shook our heads. "She wasn't there. Araneae was alone."

"When we found her," Mason began, "she didn't know us. She didn't know her name was Araneae. She called herself Kennedy."

"That was her name before," Patrick said as we all began walking toward the house.

"Yeah," Mason said. He turned to Laurel. "Can you have the doctor do a drug panel on her?"

"You think she was drugged?" Laurel asked.

"I fucking think we're back to your formula."

Laurel stopped walking. "What?"

"Think about it. She didn't know us or her name, but whatever they gave her isn't working," Mason answered. "She recognized Sparrow."

Laurel's expression became puzzled and thoughtful as we

all climbed the front steps. The air cooled within the entry as we paraded into the kitchen. I peered over the long table and out the kitchen windows. The house was no longer wide open. The air ducts had been scoured and the windows and doors secured.

Patrick was speaking quietly to Madeline. Her head was shaking, but she was smiling. His hand went to her enlarged midsection just before she laid her hand on top of his. These were the moments the rest of Chicago didn't know or see. They knew Patrick as the negotiator and dealmaker he was. They knew him to be truthful, tough, and even ruthless. They knew him as a man who made difficult decisions and met the consequences with determination.

My thoughts went to Lorna. Instead of feeding my fear, I imagined the two of us back in our apartment. From the moment we met, we shared a surreal connection. We were comfortable with one another in a way I'd never imagined. There were no awkward moments, no uncertainty. Watching Patrick with Madeline made me realize how much I envied what they were about to do, to raise a child together.

The world we lived in was cruel and unforgiving. Yet, alone with our family—our tower family—we were more than a part of the Sparrow outfit. We were friends, lovers, and partners. Soon, some of us would be parents.

"Didn't she?" Mason asked. "Reid."

I turned to him, certain my thoughts had taken me away from part of this conversation. "I'm sorry. What?"

Laurel came forward and reached for my hand. "Sit down,

Reid. Can I get you something? Maybe something to drink or eat?"

Following her lead, I sat. "I'm fine." I looked at Mason who had taken the seat across the table. "What were you saying?"

"How much sleep have you gotten in the last...going on three days?"

"Shut the fuck up. What were you asking?"

He sat back, crossing his arms over his chest. "Tell Laurel about finding Araneae."

At the mention of her name, I looked around the kitchen. "Is she upstairs?"

Patrick and Madeline came to the table. Madeline carried a pitcher of ice water and Patrick had a tray of glasses. They sat them in the middle of the table. Madeline spoke, "Yes, Sterling took her upstairs. The doctor brought an ultrasound as well as some other supplies."

"Um," I began, thinking back, "we were flying and I saw something flash. It was like a compact mirror used to signal a plane."

"Araneae had her purse?" Madeline asked.

"No." I smiled at the memory. "It turns out it was her huge fucking rock of a ring."

Everyone grinned.

"Yeah," I said. "It's the only thing that makes sense. Anyway, we landed and began walking toward where we saw the flash. As you saw, she's sunburned, and even though she drank some water, she's probably dehydrated."

I reached for the pitcher and poured myself a glass.

"I wonder how long she's been out there." Laurel said. "Tell me about her name. I feel like I should understand."

"She referred to herself as Kennedy," I offered. "It was her name—before."

"Hasn't it been Araneae since before she and Sterling married?" Laurel asked.

We all nodded.

"Which has been nearly three years?"

"Yes," Patrick answered.

Madeline sipped a glass of water. "Are you saying that she didn't know her own name or either of you?"

"No, she didn't," Mason answered. "But, she didn't seem frightened. She seemed confused."

Laurel stood and began walking back and forth by the table and breakfast bar. "But she knew Sterling."

"She did, which is odd," I said. "Because Mason told her that her husband brought the doctor here, and she seemed..." I paused to think. "I can't come up with a better word than confused."

"But as soon as he reached for her and lifted her, she knew him," Mason added.

Laurel nodded with a grin. "That's amazing."

"Amazing?" I questioned.

"What are you thinking?" Patrick asked.

"If she was given anything similar to my formula, its purpose is to mute traumatic memories. The problem from the beginning of my research has been the concern over erasing all memories." Laurel stopped and turned to all of us, her blue eyes wide. "Don't you see?"

I shook my head. "I'm sorry, Laurel, I'm not connecting the dots."

"Reid, think about it from a scientific viewpoint. Mason said he thinks this has to do with my research. You all," she was talking to us, "said you were afraid the kidnappers were coming for me. I hate to admit it, but if this is connected to my formula, I agree. So for the sake of argument, let's say all that has happened is about my research. I want to know the compound of whatever formula Araneae was given."

"If not all memories were erased for the last three years, why didn't she know us?" I asked.

Laurel moved her head from side to side. "You have to understand, I'm hypothesizing. I don't have the clinical data. Considering the empirical evidence, we can assume that she's coming out of a recent traumatic event—the kidnapping."

I nodded.

"Whatever they gave her took her mind back to a calmer time."

"When she was Kennedy," Patrick said.

"Right."

"Why then did she recognize Sparrow?" Mason asked.

Laurel's smile grew. "That's the truly amazing part. Whatever they gave her, if they did, didn't block him. Because no matter how others see Sterling, Araneae sees him as her husband, the man she loves. Her mind doesn't associate anything traumatic with him. Whatever is within the formula they probably gave her, they're on to something."

We all turned at the sound of heavy footsteps coming from the floor above. Hurriedly, Sparrow came around the corner. His expression was a conglomeration of emotions.

Laurel spoke first, "Is she okay? What about the baby?"

REID

*A*s the evening sun saturated the kitchen, we all stared, waiting for Sparrow's response.

"The baby's heartbeat is strong and there's movement."

Everyone in the room let out a collective breath.

"Araneae?" Laurel asked.

Sparrow's expression cracked. A shimmer of light gleamed in his dark eyes as his lips turned upward. "Fucking amazing. So damn strong and resilient. She's hooked up to a saline IV and asking for food."

"What does she remember?"

The luster disappeared as his head shook. "Nothing." He turned to me. "I'm sorry. Right now, that includes anything in the recent past with Lorna. Her last memories are in Chicago. She's confused about everything, even why we're here. The last two weeks are" —he shrugged— "gone."

Laurel looked from Sparrow to Mason and back. "There's no way to know yet if the amnesia is permanent. We all know that the loss of memories can be temporary."

"I don't know what happened to my wife," Sparrow said, the tendons in his neck tightening as the vein in his forehead pulsated with building pressure. "I know I have her back and someone is going to die for what they did." He let out a breath. "I also wonder if it might be better for her not to remember?"

I stood. "If she knows anything that could find Lorna—"

"Yes," he interrupted. "I get that. I just don't want her..." His words trailed away.

Laurel lifted her hands. "It's not our decision anyway, even yours, Sterling. It's up to Araneae. It's up to her mind what and when she'll remember. I'd be glad to talk with her. I might be able to prompt the return of memories."

He shook his head. "First, she needs to heal. I've contacted Marianne. The plane is heading here and then back to Chicago tonight."

"What the fuck?" My volume rose. "I'm not leaving without Lorna."

"We don't know where she is," Sparrow answered.

"But we might," Mason said, looking at me, his tone filled with optimism. "I've been thinking. Maybe we don't know exactly, but we should be closer. Reid, you have the satellite images of the ranch recording?"

The fog of worry and sleeplessness began to dissipate with my brother-in-law's question. "Yes."

"So we have the last forty-eight hours of every acre?"

Energy similar to that brought on by much-needed nutrients surged through my bloodstream. "Fuck yes. We might be able to see the vehicle that brought Araneae onto the edge of the property. That information will get us closer to Lorna."

"Reid, I'm not leaving Montana to leave Lorna," Sparrow clarified. "I'm getting my wife and child back to Chicago. According to Garrett, the same minor incidents that prompted us to leave are still happening there, but here" —he motioned around— "is too far from medical treatment." He swallowed, his Adam's apple bobbing. "I'm not asking or even fucking suggesting you make a choice between Lorna and Sparrow. I did that once. I won't do it again. I get it. I fucking get it because my wife is upstairs suffering first- and second-degree burns, dehydration, possible infection from the insect bites and various cuts and bruises on her hands and feet, with God knows what drugs in her system that may or may not be affecting my child. At this moment" —his hand went through his already-unruly hair— "I have to choose her."

I nodded. "I understand." I did. "My wife could be suffering all the same ailments. I, however, don't have a child to worry about." I turned to Patrick and Madeline, now standing together near the kitchen counter. "You two do. You have a child back in Chicago and one on the way. You should go back to Chicago too."

Patrick stood taller, but before he commented, his blue-eyed gaze went to Madeline as he spoke to her. "He's right."

Instead of answering her husband, she took a few steps until she was right before me. "Ruby is safe. We know that. I don't want to leave you here alone."

I reached for her hand and feigned a smile. I was about to say I was fine staying by myself. Her priority was to Ruby and the child she is carrying.

Before I could, Mason spoke, "He won't be alone. Laurel and I are staying."

"Laurel would be safer in Chicago," Sparrow said. "We all have reason to believe she was the target."

"We'll keep five of the capos," Mason said, not opening the subject up for discussion. "Reid and I have reconfigured the security. The satellite images are waiting. We'll follow the leads we have." He looked at his wife and forced a grin. "Doc is strong and smart. She'll help us."

"Laurel, the offer stands?" Sparrow asked.

Laurel reached for Mason's arm. "I respectfully decline. First and foremost, my place is with Mason, and if he's okay with me staying here and helping in any way to find Lorna, I will. Besides, I can run programs on Araneae's toxicology screening and anything else you need from here." Her smile bloomed. "And we both know that these two could use a hand."

Sparrow's gaze went to Mason's who nodded. "Fine, Patrick, check in with Marianne. It will take her a couple hours to get the plane ready, get the crew together, and make it here. Let her know who will be on the flight. Also, I want Renita or someone Renita trusts with her life on the plane to fly back with us. Once we're to Chicago, I'm fucking turning the tower into an obstetrics ward."

Out of the corner of my eye, I believed I saw Madeline roll her eyes. When I turned toward her, she smiled and reached for Patrick's arm. "I would have stayed."

I poured more water in my glass. "Sometimes what's best is not always the same for everyone. Honestly, I'll feel better about you and little Reid being back in Chicago."

Madeline's eyes went to her husband.

"Shouldn't we at least pretend his name is Patrick?" Patrick asked.

"We wouldn't need to pretend at all if you'd tell us," Laurel joked, easing a bit of the tension.

I lifted the glass of water as a bit of a toast. "Safe travels. We don't need any other concerns. Please let us know when you're back in Chicago and in the tower. Mason and I" —I looked at my sister-in-law— "and Laurel will be here, doing what we do best. Before you know it, we'll be back in Chicago with Lorna."

Sparrow took a step toward Mason and me. "I'm fucking holding you to that. I need you all back in Chicago." His gaze went around the kitchen. "We all need you back."

"If Araneae remembers anything..." I said.

"You'll be the first one I call."

Moving around the others, I made my way to the archway leading to the living room on my way to Mason and Laurel's office. The sun shone beyond the large windows as if it was midday, but it wasn't. Night was approaching. Dusk was near.

From the kitchen I heard Laurel ask Sparrow what she could get Araneae in the way of food or drink. My mind went to the satellite images, not listening for his answer.

Mason followed a step behind me. I wasn't sure why I hadn't thought of the images, but he was right. We should be able to find video of Araneae being left near the property line. The satellite didn't cut off at the end of the property. We could see for a few miles in all directions.

Mason and I were partway down the corridor, when Sparrow stopped us. "Hey." We both turned as he came closer. "Don't go off half-cocked."

Mason grinned. "You know me better than that."

"That's why I'm worried. I'm not stupid."

"No one—" I began.

"Your security system," Sparrow interrupted. "I know it's the best because the best minds I know created it. The kidnappers took two women in a planned operation. That points to Laurel as their target. Now, with whatever drug was given to Araneae, this is all pointing toward..." He looked directly at Mason. "Are you going to say it—to me—or are you going to keep trying to hide it, talking all quiet and private and shit?"

"The Order," Mason said, his jaw clenched. "I don't want to fucking say it because I don't want to believe it. You were there, Sparrow. You were there in the room. We made a deal."

"Don't even fucking think about going to them alone."

"He won't," I said.

Sparrow's eyes closed and opened. "Find Lorna. Get her

home where she belongs. Then fill me in on everything you know. I'll support you. Don't do anything behind my back."

Mason's neck straightened. "Lorna is our first priority."

"Keep me up to date on every damn thing."

"We will," I said.

Mason and I were silent as we walked the rest of the way down the long hallway, and Sparrow went the other direction. Once we were inside the office, we both sighed.

"First things first," I said, sitting in front of the computer I'd deemed as mine. "Give me five minutes and I'll have the satellite images."

LORNA

Though my head was on the pillow of the lower bunk, the incessant ringing refused to stop. It went on and on, much like a fire alarm, the one with the flashing lights and horrible sound. I covered my head with the other pillow, yet it wouldn't still. It wouldn't even dull.

My eyes barely opened.

The strobing light continued.

It had been going on for what could be days, weeks...My ability to rationally think was lost to the noise and flashing.

It began the morning the woman came to demand my answer.

"Your time is up," she'd said, entering the then-silent room.

A step behind her, Jet carried a tray. I didn't know its

contents, yet I wanted it. I needed it. The food in the interrogation room had been my last meal.

She sneered. "Come on, Lorna. This is your chance to be someone, to make a difference. Do we save your friend? Do we let her live?"

I am someone.

It was a voice in my head. I didn't say it aloud, but I clung to its meaning.

I was.

Someone.

"Yes, she lives," I answered.

"So your choice is Laurel. She's the one who will suffer."

I shook my head. "No, I won't give you an answer to that. Neither one of them should suffer. Both should live."

She turned and nodded to Jet who left with the tray. "You disappoint me, Lorna Pierce."

"My name is Lorna Murray."

"Born a no one and doomed to die the same. I suppose that's your choice." She turned on her heels, leaving me alone.

Nearly a minute later, Jet returned. He no longer carried the tray. Instinctively, I took a step back, preparing for his abuse such as before. Perhaps it would be a punishment for my answer.

I stood straighter, finding strength.

Fuck them.

I wouldn't sell out my friends, no matter what he did.

My concentration was on his face, his expression. I didn't see what he had in his grasp. The tiny object didn't register.

Until it did.

A small syringe.

"No, wait," I pleaded. "What is that?"

More steps backward.

I backed away until there was nowhere to go. Trapped between the concrete blocks and this muscular tall man, I did what I could do. I fought.

A knee to his groin.

The heel of my hand to his nose.

Those were the moves Mason taught me long ago.

In all my thirty-five years, I'd never used one of his self-defense maneuvers. There was never the need.

As soon as I delivered the kick to his groin, I knew it was ineffective. I was too short to make a full impact.

The heel of my hand hit hard, causing blood to spew as Jet took a staggering step backward.

I did what I could do.

I ran.

The open door was right before me.

My forward momentum reversed as my scalp screamed out in pain. With a fist full of my hair, he pulled me backward before shoving me. I had just enough time to catch myself with my hands as I landed face-first upon the concrete floor. Jet's weight landed on top of me, expelling the air from my lungs and pushing my hips into the hard floor. Warmth oozed down my scalp and neck.

It took a few seconds to realize it was his blood saturating my hair as he held my arm in place and injected the contents of the syringe.

"Bitch," he spewed in my ear. "I should fuck you."

Though I used all my strength, he was stronger. I kicked and twisted, yet he rolled me to my back with ease. Straddling my waist, he pinned my wrists above my head, holding them with one of his hands. Evil and hatred emanated from his gaze as he wiped the blood coming from his nose. I had no idea what I'd done to deserve the loathing he displayed. Maybe nothing. Maybe simply by being.

"Stop," I screamed as loud as I could.

"Would you rather take me in your ass?" His lips curled in a menacing sneer. "Say the word, bitch, and I'll roll you back over."

My heart raged against my breastbone, and white spots appeared before my eyes. I continued to scream, uncertain if anyone could hear or care.

As he gripped the waist of my pants, I thrashed as much as possible. At the same time, I searched for moisture, conjuring up all the saliva I could, and spat in his face.

My head reeled as his hand contacted my cheek.

I gasped for breath as I continued to fight.

The blows continued.

Sometime during the assault, he'd freed my hands. I could use them to shield my face, yet I couldn't get free. A punch slammed into my stomach seconds before he grabbed my waistbands and pulled down my pants and panties in one fluid movement.

I screamed again, kicking as he reached for his belt and loosened the buckle.

"I'm so sorry, Reid." It was my thought as I faced reality.

I couldn't fight anymore. There was no place for me to go.

It was at that moment I heard Jet's name.

His jaw tightened, the cords in his neck pulling taut, as his gaze went from me to over my head.

In hindsight, I should have done something, anything, but my energy was gone.

Jet fastened his buckle and stood. Before he was fully erect, he leaned over and spat.

I closed my eyes as his saliva and whatever else he'd conjured forward landed upon my face, combining with his blood.

Breathing heavily, I lay frozen upon the floor until the door closed.

During the ordeal I hadn't cried.

I wasn't sure why I hadn't, but that was before.

As I reached for my panties and slacks still on my ankles, the tears came. The sheer terror combined with humiliation and exhaustion. My entire body trembled to the point of convulsions. Now fully clothed, I crawled toward the bunk bed and wiped my face with the blanket. Then up to my knees, I folded my arms and lowered my head to the bunk, uncertain if I had the energy to stand.

My eyes closed as sobs resonated from my chest and then it began.

The small room filled with the awful high-pitched squeal

as the light above was lost to flashing coming from a small casing high above. I searched for reasons—perhaps the building was on fire.

No one came.

Over time, I made my way to the small sink and washed the blood and spit from my battered face. I tenderly touched the swollen flesh. My eyelids, cheeks, and lips were all enlarged and sore to the touch. I leaned forward, fighting dizziness, and washed the blood that I could from my hair. My scalp too was painful. Finally, I climbed back into the bed and covered my head.

With my eyes covered and closed, the strobing light was diminished, yet nothing could lessen the ear-piercing squeal.

The screech didn't stop.

It hadn't.

I was uncertain of how much time had come and gone.

My only source of water was the faucet on the small sink.

Food was gone.

Araneae was gone.

The woman was gone.

Even Jet was gone.

I was trapped in a gray box as the light strobed, as the alarm continued its scream.

I tried to sleep. I prayed to sleep.

There were moments, I couldn't be certain of how long, that reality slipped away and I was somewhere else.

Were they dreams?

Were they wishes?

Was it the afterlife?

I couldn't be sure, but as time dragged on in this incessant hell, I also prayed for that.

If I stopped drinking water, would death come sooner?

Thoughts were difficult to link together.

Rational thought left me as I slid deeper and deeper into despair.

Memories returned of my life.

Maybe I was dying. They say that your life flashes before your eyes.

My memories weren't a flash, but a slow slideshow.

Not every scene was pretty or worth recalling.

I had the sensation of motion.

The ringing finally ended, or my mind had snapped and my hearing was gone.

My swollen eyelids painfully fluttered with the sense that I was no longer alone.

When my eyes focused, the gray room was gone.

I stared up at the sky churning with clouds.

This wasn't real, but maybe it was the peace that came with death.

Yet with time, the dream or hallucination became realer. The ground beneath my battered body gained substance. My fingernails clawed into the packed dirt. Nerve endings came to life with the sensation of a million ants, their small legs scurrying over my skin and bites.

Bites.

I hurried to stand, my sore muscles screaming as I

brushed my legs and arms. Whether real or imaginary, I could feel their presence on my skin. I ripped my shirt from my body and then my pants. I'd tried so hard to keep my clothes on, and now I wanted them off. My body ached as I danced the primal dance of ridding my body of unwanted visitors.

Once I had cleared them away, the world seemed clearer. The clouds continued to build, obscuring a star-peppered dark sky. The cool air kissed my skin as I shook out my top and again pulled it over my head.

And then as the fabric came away from my eyes, like the ripping of a veil, I saw her.

With the hard ground assaulting my tender feet, I moved toward the figure.

"Araneae?"

Was she real or part of this nightmare?

As I drew closer, I was certain that whoever she was, she was of the female persuasion.

I peered all around at the sky, open land, and dried grass. The howl of carnivorous creatures floated through the night. "Where are we?"

The person didn't answer.

She didn't speak.

Her knees were drawn up to her chin as she leaned in the darkness against a large rock. A new breeze blew my hair and skirted over my bare legs. I crossed my arms over my chest and took a small step toward her.

Every movement hurt.

Every inch of my body ached.

Pressing my lips together and trying not to limp, I made my way to the woman and laid my hand on her bony knee. "Are you all right?"

A cloud shifted high above. The terrain around us illuminated with eerie blue moonlight.

"Hello," I tried once more.

Her skinny arms surrounding her bony knees appeared skeletal-like. Her hands gripping her legs were frail. Even in the blue light, I could make out the veins and bones through flesh that was too thin. This woman needed food.

"I can help you."

I couldn't. I didn't know where we were, but I wanted to help her.

She turned toward me.

As her face came into view, I gasped.

Though her hair was a ghostly pale shade of red, her sunken eyes were a vibrant green.

"Who are you?" I demanded.

Her chin rose as she laughed—cackled such as a witch from a child's horror movie. "I told them" —her voice was weak in comparison to her cackle— "all I knew about you."

My feet backed away as I struggled not to trip. "Please tell me who you are."

"You know me, Lorna."

My pulse raced as I tried to make sense of what was happening.

I shook my head from side to side. "I don't know you."

"Yes, you do."

"No." I protested.

"I'm nobody. I've always been nobody."

A cold chilled covered my skin. My feet no longer ached. My battered face no longer registered. My question stayed for a moment on the tip of my tongue. Finally, I made the words go forth. "Are you me?"

REID

Earlier the same day

*T*he last twenty-four hours passed in the blink of an eye. Sparrow, Araneae, Patrick, and Madeline were all back and safe in Chicago, behind the protective shield of our tower. I didn't have time to give them more thought than that. They were there. Both women were being monitored as were their unborn babies. Their world was once again right.

Unlike mine.

We'd found the satellite images we'd wanted.

Early Saturday morning, a dusty old black Ford truck entered the far west portion of Mason's land, coming from a small intrastate highway. A man wearing a baseball cap, jeans, and worn jacket carried an object from the truck—an object we believed to be Araneae.

While that was good news, it wasn't enough. A man fitting that description was not specific enough. We couldn't get close enough for any facial recognition software. As for the truck, there was only one visible license plate, on the rear of the truck. No matter what we did to the picture, we couldn't make it out. Since there was no front plate, we could assume that the truck came from one of the states that only required rear plates.

At this moment in time, there were nineteen such states.

None were west of Montana.

We had the make and model.

The sheer number of F-250 black Ford trucks made in 2010 made that information useless. Finding the one truck that had driven onto the ranch was like a needle in a haystack. Even when we limited the number to the nineteen states that didn't require a front license plate, the number was astronomical.

And then it occurred to me. The truck left the property headed west, the same direction as the helicopter. We began running programs accessing traffic cameras cross-referenced with towns, cities, and other landmarks accessible to the west. I started with the smaller towns.

Not all of them had traffic cameras.

However, due to the vast expanse of Montana's highways, the state had recently added cameras and call booths along the long stretches of interstate. There were also cameras when entering and exiting state and national parks and forests. The larger cities such as Butte and Missoula were much easier.

Thankfully, we had a time stamp to follow.

The truck left the property Saturday morning at 8:23 a.m. headed west.

Early this morning, nearly twenty-four hours after Araneae had been left, we found what we believe was the same truck. It traveled through Butte and beyond. We could now see that the man was Caucasian with black hair. Again, that was too broad, the images too grainy for any kind of recognition. The truck then disappeared from Interstate 90 north of Highway 1.

Mason immediately dispatched two of the Sparrow capos toward Anaconda. Outside of the city—also the county seat— the land was rugged. The elevations made for excellent snow skiing when the weather cooled. The terrain was covered in untamed forestlands and dotted with lakes.

Our progress had brought to life budding optimism tempered by reality. Our haystack was smaller, but the needle was still fucking small.

All of our wives willingly wore trackers sewn into all of their handbags and shoes. Each was a GPS transmitter equipped for one purpose: to transmit the location.

We'd determined the ladies hadn't had time to take their purses, but they did leave with our failsafe alternative—shoes —because who wouldn't always have their shoes? As soon as we reached the ranch, I began running a program to locate their transmission.

Unfortunately, as soon as it was found, it was determined that it had stopped relaying rather quickly after their kidnapping. The last transmission was still within the bounds of the ranch. Since the only way to stop the transmission was to contain the transmitter—shoes—in a box lined with a special polymer, we'd assumed the shoes had been destroyed.

I'd forgotten about that program, leaving it running in the background. It had been useless and well, my mind was in a million places.

The program dinged Sunday evening at exactly 8:07 p.m.

The tracers were reactivated.

"What the fuck?" Mason said, hitting keys and bringing the GPS to one of the screens. "It's Lorna's and Araneae's trackers. They're broadcasting from the same spot."

I stepped closer. "Where?"

Mason enlarged the map. "Elevation eight thousand feet. West-southwest of Anaconda."

"I'm calling Christian." Christian was the Sparrow capo in charge of the search party we'd deployed that direction earlier in the day. Once I completed my call, I stared back at the map. "They're less than an hour out."

Mason shook his head. "It doesn't make sense. Why would the trackers suddenly start to transmit?"

"I don't know why they stopped."

The strain of the last few days showed on my brother-in-law's face. "Unless the kidnappers knew what polymer was needed."

"Very few would—"

"The Order would."

The muscles in my neck and back tightened. We could take down a warring outfit, cartel, or bratva. We had. The more signs pointing toward the Order, the more worried for my wife I became.

Mason's green gaze came to me. "I don't like it. It's a trap."

He was probably right. Unless he wasn't.

"So what? We don't go after our first real clue to save Lorna?"

"No, of course we do."

I emphasized each phrase. "Her shoes are there. I'm not leaving this stone unturned. My wife could still be there."

"If she ever was," Mason stood and paced the length of the office. His colorful arms flexed as his long legs moved step by step and his boots clipped the hard-surface floor.

"I fucking want to go myself," I admitted, the stress coursing through my circulation making it difficult to stay focused.

"Even if we used my plane, the capos are closer." The tension had oozed from his expression and was now thick in Mason's voice. It hung in the air around us like a thick, choking cloud as we both stared at the satellite image.

Trees.

That was all I fucking saw—trees. As I stared, I recognized that they were predominantly pines. Montana's state tree was the ponderosa pine. Some measured up to two hundred and twenty feet high and eight feet in diameter. It made sense. Pine trees of any variety made the best cover because unlike deciduous trees, pines never lost their needles, not in a way to disclose this hideout.

We were back at our keyboards when at 9:34 p.m. my phone rang. Mason's eyes met mine.

The screen read *Christian*.

"Are you there? Tell me what you have," I demanded as the call connected.

"We are here. We're not sure what this place is." Before I could ask, he went on, "It's a compound. I'm sending pictures, but it's beginning to get dark. Not completely. You know, this fucking weird dusk."

I put the phone on speaker. "Christian, describe what you found so far."

"The coordinates you gave us were, well, inaccessible. And then we found this road. Fuck, it's not a road. It's one lane up a mountain."

"Get to the damned point," I pushed.

"Christian," Mason began, his tone calmer. "Is anyone there?"

"I can't be sure, Mr. Pierce. It appears abandoned. I'd say recently abandoned. There are fresh tire tracks. While I can't confirm with just visual evidence, I'd say the tire tracks were made by a truck."

"Anything else."

"Yeah, about half a mile away to the east is a clearing, the perfect place to land a helicopter."

I was no longer seated, but standing and pacing by the

computers in Mason's office while he was hitting keys, bringing the satellite image closer.

"Look over here." Mason moved the cursor to what appeared to be a clearing in the trees.

"Are you sure no one is there?" I asked.

"We called you before doing a sweep. The buildings look a bit like power stations. You know, all made of concrete blocks. They aren't big, at least not on the ground level."

"Protect yourselves," Mason said. "Are your vests in place?"

"Yes, sir."

"Wait," I said, going to the keyboard and bringing up the tracker program. "Christian, turn your GPS on, the one on your phone."

Mason's eyes met mine as we watched the two signals.

"Mrs. Murray's and Mrs. Sparrow's tracker signals are one hundred and twelve feet south-southeast."

"Sir, the buildings are the other way."

Mason stood and spoke quietly. "I'm not losing capos to the Order. The Order doesn't leave breadcrumbs it doesn't expect to have followed."

My heart ached with the thought of Lorna in one of the buildings Christian described.

Had they left her alone?

What was the plan?

Mason spoke, "I want you and Romero to get back from the buildings. Make sure that your vehicle is at least one hundred yards away."

"Sir?"

"You're not going to open the doors—not yet. Instead, I want you to shoot six inches above each door handle. Can you do that?"

"From one hundred yards?" Christian asked.

"I can, sir," a second voice said.

"Romero, listen carefully," Mason said. "I fucking hope I'm wrong, but if not, you need to listen very carefully. I've set explosives like what I'm imagining could be waiting for you."

Booby traps.

"Sir, what if Mrs. Murray...?"

Romero didn't need to finish the sentence. Mason and I both knew what would happen.

"There's a chance," Mason continued, "that only one building is rigged. I can't explain the logic right now; I just know it's a possibility. Get farther away and take cover if you can. Leave the phone on. The satellite is delayed. We'll be able to hear before we see."

Mason and I waited as they followed his instruction, moving their vehicle and taking cover.

"Sir, we're set."

My pulse raced to the point of nausea as I imagined Lorna inside one of those buildings. In the seconds that followed, I said prayers to every Supreme Being, even asking my father I lost too young and my mother and grandmother to reach down from heaven and protect the woman I loved.

"Do it," Mason said.

Rapid gunfire came through the speaker.

And nothing.

"Sir, nothing happened with the first building."

"You're not done yet," Mason said.

Rapid gunfire again.

A deafening explosion.

My breath caught in my chest. "Romero, Christian, are you all right?"

REID

The sound of the blast reverberated through the office.

"Christian. Romero?" Mason screamed into the phone. He looked up at me. "The fucking line went dead."

We both turned to the real-time, albeit delayed, satellite image as a flash and a plume of smoke came from between the trees. My heart sank in my chest. "What if she was in there?"

Mason's head shook. "If she was, she wasn't getting out."

My steps staggered as I reached for the desk chair and my knees gave out. My sorrow quickly morphed to rage. I shot out of the chair, sending it flying behind me. "Lorna wasn't in there." My voice rose. "She wasn't. There's no way. I will fucking take down the whole goddamned Order."

As Mason came toward me, I stared him down. "No. Don't fucking try to stop me."

He lifted his hands. "I'm not."

My gaze searched the room around us. I had an unmet need to lash out, to hit, and to destroy. It bubbled within me from a simmering fury to a boiling rage. Turning away I stomped down the corridor toward the front of the house. I didn't know where I was going or what I was seeking, but the small slice of humanity still within me said whatever I sought wasn't inside. I wouldn't find refuge in destroying Mason and Laurel's home.

I flung open the tall wooden front door.

Like my emotions, the darkening sky was a simmering caldron of swirling gray clouds. Some hung low over the mountain peaks in the distance with shades of red decorating their undersides as rays of the setting sun shone upward. Others churned high above.

My steps led me out to the closest outbuilding.

I pulled open the door, searching.

For what, I didn't know.

And then I saw it. In the diminishing light, leaning against a corner was a wooden baseball bat.

It didn't matter to me who it belonged to.

I moved forward until it was in my grasp. My knuckles blanched as I gripped the handle and turned back outside to the dusk. A hundred yards away was the fence that contained one of the corrals. There were no horses up this way. There hadn't been since we'd arrived. The ranch hands had them out on the property.

My mind focused on the baseball bat in my grasp.

I'd never been interested in sports.

When I was a kid, while other boys made a name for themselves on the football or baseball fields or basketball court, my nose was in a book. Whether it was math, science, or history, I couldn't get enough. The coaches saw my height and the way my body matured. They watched as I took the mandatory gym class or weight training. They encouraged me to try out for this sport or for that. They told me stories of all-star athletes and the grandeur of six- and seven-digit salaries.

Coming from a modest beginning, I'd be lying if I said they didn't make it sound appealing.

I talked to my mother and grandmother and told them what the coaches said.

They didn't dismiss the offers. Instead, they told me that life was an offer.

Did I want to spend it doing something that didn't appeal to me, simply because I could?

If I truly wanted the life the coaches described, wouldn't it be more rewarding if I accomplished it doing what I loved?

"I did it," I called out into the wind to the ghosts of my ancestors. "And now that life took her. I don't fucking care about the money or the houses." My stomach threatened to revolt as I screamed at the clouds. "I only care about Lorna."

My attention went back to the bat in my hand. I gripped the handle as tight as I could and brought it back.

My anger, frustration, and grief materialized in the form of a six-inch-diameter fence post. I set my stance and swung.

The bat struck the post. The impact reverberated through the bat to my grip. I veered back and struck it again. Each strike was harder than the last. Finally, the bat gave up. I was left with the handle of a splintered bat in my hand.

"Reid?"

I turned to see Laurel walking toward me. My head shook as my frustration came to life in the form of tears blurring my vision of the woman coming my way. "Don't, Laurel."

She stopped. Her long hair and dress were blowing in the breeze as the clouds continued to build. "Mason said to tell you that Christian and Romero are all right."

Letting out a breath, I dropped the bat's handle to the ground. "I can't..."

Laurel came closer. "Nothing is for certain."

"I didn't look for her."

"Yes" —she reached out and placed her hand upon my chest— "you have. You've been searching nonstop, doing all you could do."

I laid my hand over hers. "No, I didn't look for Lorna the night we met. I never imagined that I'd find a woman to love. I wasn't trying. I had the life I wanted. I didn't think I needed more."

A tear trickled down Laurel's cheek as she smiled sadly. "But you found her."

"She blew me away." I remembered her at that stupid debutante ball in New York. We'd all been present to secure allies in our recent coup. I recalled the blue dress she wore and her gorgeous red hair pinned up with a small crown. Fuck,

I thought she was royalty. I forced a smile. "She's everything I didn't imagine needing or wanting in a miniature package."

Laurel lifted her hand, palm up. "Come back inside." She looked down at the broken bat. "I guess we'll get Seth's kids a new bat."

"Oh" —I looked down and then back up— "I didn't know."

"Come inside, Reid."

The emotions that propelled me out the door were gone, leaving me an empty shell. I didn't argue, taking my friend's hand and walking back to the sidewalk, up the stairs, and into the house.

The wood-lined entry was warm with golden light, yet I felt only the chill.

"You've barely slept," Laurel said as she closed the front doors.

Beyond the windows, rain began to fall.

"Can I get you something to eat? How about a sandwich?"

"Reid," Mason called, "get your ass back down here."

With a quick glance toward Laurel, I took off, nearly running through the entry, living room, and corridor. Once I crossed the threshold of the office, I stopped. "What?"

"Look at this."

I stared up at the screen. The image was grainy as natural light was waning. "Fuck." My heart remembered how to beat as it took on a double-time rhythm. "That's the same fucking truck."

"At about the same spot we found Araneae."

"Can you see what they're doing? Is it Lorna?"

"I can't get that close," Mason said. "But this time, he carried two objects."

"Okay." My mind was fully revived. "Get the plane, we're headed over there."

Mason rushed past me. A second later, he came to a dead stop. The large raindrops pelting the windows came into range like the sounding of war drums. Before us, the plates of glass blurred as the brewing storm came into view. "It's fucking raining."

"So what?" I asked. "Planes fly in rain all the damn time."

"Big planes." His green gaze came to me. "I'll check the radar."

Laurel entered from the other direction with her phone in her hand. "Storms. They're coming from the south. Dubois is recording fifteen lightning strikes per minute."

"No." My head shook. "We have to get there. What if she's there? What if she wasn't in that building?" A thought came to mind. "I know." I grabbed Mason's shirt. "The explosion, it was for you. It was a trick to get you to go after her. The Order, they want Laurel and the way to get her is to eliminate you."

Mason took a deep breath and pulled my grip from his clothes. "We'll take the truck."

"It will take too long."

"What fucking choice do we have?" he countered.

"Where are the capos?" Laurel asked, a calming voice in the storm.

"Near Anaconda," I said.

"Ranch hands?" she asked.

"I'd have to contact Seth," Mason answered.

"Let's go in the truck," she said.

"Laurel, you don't..." I didn't finish.

Her blue eyes came to me as they had outside. "I stayed to help. I'm not a medical doctor, but I know a few things. Let me grab the first-aid kit and I'll meet you both out front." She looked at Mason. "Make sure the tank is full. We're not stopping." With that she turned and headed for the stairs.

When I looked back at Mason, I grinned. "She's good for you."

He nodded. "And Lorna is for you. Come on, we're getting my sister back."

When I stepped outside, I stared at Mason's truck. It was bigger than a normal truck, and there was an ATV loaded in the long bed.

"What's that for?"

"In case we need it."

I nodded.

As we all piled into the truck, Mason driving, me riding shotgun—literally, we were carrying—and Laurel in the back seat, I called Romero. He answered right away.

"We need you to head back this way. The truck was just spotted in the same area where Mrs. Sparrow was found."

"Sir, we entered the one building."

I put the phone on speaker as Mason fired up the engine,

and we headed down the long lane toward the main roads. "Why?"

"I told him to," Mason said. "The booby trap was already sprung."

"What did you find?" My elation began to slip away. "Who did you find?"

"No *who*, Mr. Murray. This place was...fuck, there were two cells on a floor underground. Like actual jail cells—no bars, but doors that lock, beds, toilet, and sink."

My stomach twisted. "Did you find anything in them?"

"No personal possessions. They were both...well, both looked as if they'd been recently occupied. And we found blood splatter on the floor in one. It seemed recent."

My eyes closed as I tried to rein in whatever fucking emotions were going through me.

"We'll text you the exact coordinates of where Mrs. Sparrow was found," Mason said. "If you get close first, call while you still have cell service."

After the call ended, I leaned back against the door and seat. Big fat raindrops pummeled the windshield as the headlights cut through the darkness.

REID

At nearly midnight, we were three miles from our destination when Mason's phone rang. Christian's name appeared on the dashboard screen. The three of us exchanged glances as Mason hit the green icon.

"Talk to us," he said.

"We are about there. Cell service is spotty and the rain is coming down."

"Do you see anyone?"

"No, not yet. We have our flashlights. I have you on Bluetooth."

Fuck, cell service didn't work the other day. "Aran—Mrs. Sparrow," I said, trying to keep my voice calm, "was near a large rock south of the road. Keep talking to us."

"I see the rock," Christian said. "We're walking that way."

"Over here," Romero yelled from a distance.

"Fuck, I see them," Christian said.

Them?

"They look..." Static filled the line just before we lost his signal.

Mason's gaze went between the poor excuse for a road and me. "Don't jump to fucking conclusions."

"They?"

He shook his head.

I couldn't speak. My jaw clenched as I glared straight ahead.

The next two miles took hours or days. That was the way they seemed until we finally caught sight of the capos' car. My pulse thumped in my veins as my fingers itched to free myself from the truck. It was the headlights shining through the darkness and illuminating the large rock that became clear.

Mason brought the truck to a stop, seconds after I had the door open.

What had been hard, dry ground yesterday morning was slick and wet. Rain saturated my hair and clothes. My boots sank in the deepening mud, splattering my jeans as I ran toward their car.

Christian and Romero were soaking wet, standing beside the open back doors.

"Where is she?" I called, reaching the car a few seconds before Mason.

Within the back seat was not one but two women, both unconscious.

I didn't concentrate on the one I didn't know. Instinctively, I reached for my wife.

Tears came to my eyes as I laid two fingers on her neck.

A long breath escaped my lungs as I detected a pulse.

Now that I knew she was alive, I took in her battered body.

My wife's beautiful red hair was a wet, tangled mess littered with grass and twigs. I tenderly pushed rogue strands away from her battered face, running a finger gently over her dark and swollen cheeks and eyes. "Get a fucking blanket," I yelled, noticing the way her saturated shirt clung to her small frame, covering her panties. Her legs were bare and along with bruises, were covered in angry small red lesions.

Mason brought a blanket from behind the seat in his truck.

Lorna groaned as I lifted her, yet she remained unconscious.

In the illumination of the headlights, I noticed more puss-filled red dots on her arms. Her fingernails were ragged and her hands bruised. Her feet were as Araneae's had been, cut and dirty.

Mason laid the wool blanket over his sister.

"Is she?" he asked.

As I shook my head, Romero answered, "She has a pulse. It's weak."

"Bring her to the truck," Laurel said as Mason stared into the back seat of the capos' car.

"Fuck," he muttered.

My wife was as light as a feather, lighter than I remembered. Cradling her in my arms, I carried her to Mason's truck. My eyes met Laurel's. "I don't want to leave her."

"Lay her down in the back seat. I need to check her, and then you can ride in the back with her."

I nodded as I laid her gently on the seat. "What are the spots?"

"I can't be sure, but I suspect insect bites of some kind. We need to get her on an antibiotic as soon as possible. Too many bites, even from nonpoisonous insects can be..."

Deadly was the word she didn't say.

I couldn't peel my gaze away from my wife as Laurel helped her and talked with me.

Finally, I noticed Mason standing near the car and staring. His arms were crossed and his neck stiff. There was something in his demeanor. I'd expect more jubilance at finding Lorna alive. And then I remembered the stranger found with her. I walked over to my friend. "Is she..." I bent down and looked closer at the other person, placed my fingers on her neck. I did as I had done in searching for Lorna's pulse.

There was none.

Not only was she dead, but she looked as if she'd been that way for a while. Not as in decomposed, but as in emaciated. Hell, she looked like a skeleton.

"Fucking dead," Mason replied.

The dome light in the car illuminated her gaunt features, dark circles around her eyes, and thin skin. "Why does she look familiar?"

"Because she looks like Lorna," he said. Turning his stare to me, he added, "She's our mother."

LORNA

*I*t had been three days since I awoke to the sound of beeps and the handsomest, most loving gaze I'd ever known. It was as if I'd fallen asleep in his arms and awoken under his gaze. I had sparse memories of Mason and Laurel's ranch, yet nothing was solidly fixed in my recollection after our safe life in this tower.

Nearly two weeks of my life were gone or hidden by an unmovable veil.

I wasn't without clues.

My body ached in places I hadn't known existed. I had multiple broken ribs, my left cheekbone had been surgically reconstructed, and I had an appointment to have a broken tooth repaired.

My skin was covered in medical creams and still the bites over my arms, torso, and legs continued to itch. I'd lost over ten pounds, yet I had trouble keeping food down. A step or even reaching for a glass of water was painful. My temples ached from an incessant ringing in my ears that had only recently begun to fade. One look in a mirror told me that I'd lived through a nightmare—one I couldn't recall.

While the particulars of what had happened weren't in my mind, there was a looming sense of terror just outside my reality. It was with me, lingering and waiting to pounce. I couldn't see it, nor could I escape from it.

Even in the apartment where I'd lived with Reid for the last nine years, a simple noise set me on full alert. I jumped at the beep of the microwave and startled at the whistle of the tea kettle. A blinking light set my pulse racing, and perspiration dotted my brow as I tried mostly unsuccessfully to sleep.

All that I knew of my ordeal was what I could see and feel, as well as what I'd been told by Reid and the others.

Araneae and I were taken from Mason's ranch.

It was believed that we were kept in a mostly underground bunker.

We were found nearly two days apart in the same area.

If there was more to the story that anyone knew, I hadn't been told. I also hadn't pushed. The doctor said my body needed to rest and heal, and in time, my mind would catch up. The resulting black hole in time left me as uneasy as the injuries I'd suffered.

At least, I wasn't alone in my loss of recall. Araneae couldn't remember what occurred either. Our questions were met with platitudes and offers of food, drink, and rest. Reid and the others walked around both of us as if there were eggshells scattered about the floor in danger of cracking.

I spent hours peering out at the Chicago skyline and the blue of Lake Michigan, hoping that something would come back. I have sat and paced within the safe confines of our tower. The answers seem so close, yet out of reach.

"Maybe it's better this way," Araneae said, as she lay her head on the sofa and rested her hand on her growing baby bump.

The two of us were sitting in her living room, the cobalt-blue sky and waves of the great lake sparkling beyond the windows.

"I hate not remembering," I confessed.

Araneae turned to me. While her expression was filled with concern, her face had been spared the same signs of our captivity as mine.

Some of my dark bruises were lightening, turning from deep black and purple to shades of green with yellow halos. Both of our feet were affected. She had hers, covered in bandages, up on the edge of the coffee table.

"When I was younger, too young to drink," she said, "my friend Louisa and I snuck some vodka into a party. I woke up in the bathroom of her parents' house." Her head shook. "Besides puking my guts, I couldn't remember what had happened or how we'd gotten there. I hated the feeling and didn't touch alcohol for years after that."

"Even wine?" I asked with a smile.

"Well, it takes time to develop the taste for good wine."

"I'll take good wine over cheap vodka."

Araneae laughed. "I never said it was cheap."

"You were a teenager. It was probably cheap."

Private school.

I shook my head, wondering where that thought had come from. "I've never blacked out from alcohol." I said.

"Never? Even when you were young?"

"No. I was kind of boring." *Working to keep a roof over my head.* I didn't say that. "I didn't need a bad personal experience to keep me on the straight and narrow."

Araneae groaned as she leaned forward and lifted a glass of lemonade. "Oh, I wish I could take stronger painkillers."

My temples throbbed as sunlight glistened on the lake surface below. Each deep breath reminded me of the ache in my ribs. "I won't take them either."

Her eyes opened wide. "Oh, Lorna, are you...?"

I shook my head. "No. I'm not pregnant. I think we have enough pregnancy hormones in this tower for right now."

Araneae ran her finger over the condensation of the glass. "May I ask you then why you won't take the painkillers?" She looked over and grinned. "Because if I could I would with a wine chaser."

I feigned a smile. "It's no real secret. Mace and I grew up with an alcoholic, drug-addicted mother." I shrugged. "And believe it or not, those weren't her worst qualities. Anyway, I refused to follow in her footsteps even when I was younger."

"I'm sorry."

I waved my hand. "Don't be. It's old news. I haven't seen her since before my high school graduation. It's even longer for Mace." I sighed. "I'm not sure why I brought her up."

"I'm not pretending to know what that's like," Araneae said, "but I do get losing parents young. It...there's a hole."

"Your story is a lot happier."

Her light brown eyes met mine. "Lorna, we're both here, in our home, after God knows what happened. If you ask me, we both have happy endings." She laid her hand over her baby bump. "With many more stories to come."

LORNA

*L*ater that night as I settled into bed next to my husband, I turned to Reid. "I wish you knew more about what happened to us."

His deep voice overpowered the distant ringing within my ears. "Has anything come back? Do you remember anything else?"

I shook my head. "It feels like the information is close, yet I can't find it." I let out a long sigh. "You know, it's like when you lose something, yet you're sure it's right there."

Reid gently encouraged me to lay my head on his broad shoulder as he wrapped his arms around me. "I have you back." He kissed my hair.

While he was gentle, I winced at the pressure on my tender scalp.

"Sweetheart, I'm sorry."

"No, don't be." I turned my gaze to his and as my eyes adjusted to the dimness, I took in his handsome features—his loving gaze, the flawlessness of his mahogany complexion, his high cheekbones, and his strong chin. I ran my finger over his lush lips, imagining them on mine or other more sensitive places. As my insides twisted, I said, "I'll take your affection, no matter how much it hurts."

Reid's brows knitted together. "I never want you to hurt, not from me or anyone else. Whoever did this to you will pay. I promise, you're safe and they'll never hurt you again."

Sighing, I settled into the crook of his strong arm. "I don't care if they pay. I would like to know they can't do this to anyone else."

"I love you, Lorna. I didn't need to lose you to know that."

A smile crept across my face as I hugged his arm. "I love you too. I feel" —I searched for words— "...safe, secure, loved..." When our gazes met, I confessed, "When we're together, I feel like I'm somebody."

"You, Lorna Murray, are definitely somebody."

I ran my fingers over his forearm, feeling the warmth of his dark skin under my fingertips and relishing in our familiar differences. The sounds of our breathing filled our bedroom. His breaths became spaced and rhythmic, alerting me to the fact that he'd fallen asleep. Knowing my husband, I doubted that he slept much when I was gone.

Savoring the security of his embrace as well as the fresh scent of his recently showered skin, I cuddled toward his side and listened to the beat of his heart, reminding myself of my safety as I drifted into a fretful sleep.

All at once, I woke with a start.

"What is it?" Reid asked, leaning over me.

With his close proximity, the white orbs surrounding his dark eyes were all I could see in our lightless bedroom. Before I could respond, gently and reassuringly, his lush firm lips came to mine.

"Sweetheart, you're fine. You're here."

A moan came from my throat as I pushed closer, returning his kiss.

His large hands roamed down my lower back and over my behind.

Heat flooded my twisting core as I reached for his cheeks, holding his lips to mine as my tongue sought entrance, ready to dance with his.

My desire waned as a wince replaced my moan when his weight came over my ribs and bruised hip bones. My pulse quickened and breathing stalled as perspiration dotted my forehead.

Before I could analyze what had happened, Reid pulled away.

His stare penetrated mine. "No, Lorna, I won't hurt you."

"You aren't," I said, not being fully truthful. "You're loving me."

Holding his toned and hard torso above me, Reid teased a strand of my hair away from my face as he scanned my bruises. "I do and will forever love you. You are still the most beautiful woman in this world. I fucking want to show you that by bringing the head of whoever did this to your feet."

My lips curled upward. "I don't want anyone but you."

"Then I want to show you by making love all night long...but not until you're ready."

"I'm ready. I just need to be on top."

His head shook as a small grin graced his lips. "Sweetheart, I want you on top, under me, with me. Please, for now, humor me. Let me just hold you in my arms and you can tell me what caused you to wake."

I knew he was right, yet I yearned to be with him, connected in a way only we can be.

With a sigh, I settled back onto his shoulder and thought about what had awakened me. "I-I had a dream or nightmare." My body shivered. "It seemed real."

He gently rolled until his front was to my back as he held me safe in his embrace. "You're here and safe."

"It's so weird. It's like I have dreams or memories and I don't know which."

"Tell me."

"It'll sound crazy," I admitted.

"Your crazy hasn't scared me away yet. I don't think it will now"

"It's probably nothing. I was talking with Araneae today, and for some reason the subject of my mother came up."

Reid sat up, turning me back toward him. "Your mother?"

"Yeah, I know it's stupid. I mean, I haven't seen or heard from her—"

"What about your mother?"

"I was just telling Araneae why I'm hesitant to take pain pills."

"In your dream?"

"No. In the dream, my mom is...well, she was with me." My nose scrunched. "She's old, older than her years. Very thin. I guess sex and drugs weren't the best plan for a healthy life."

Reid was staring at me. "Tell me more. Did she talk to you?"

"Reid, it wasn't real. It's all the drugs they gave me, playing tricks on me. Laurel said it could happen. I'll talk more to her about it tomorrow." I scoffed. "You know, I never realized how convenient it was to have a live-in shrink."

"She's not exactly..." He kissed my forehead. "Okay, but if something comes to you."

I stared up at our ceiling, wondering how totally crazy it would sound to say the words aloud. I rolled toward my husband. "Do you promise not to laugh?"

"Laugh, no. Smile, maybe."

"Don't tell Mason. He'll think I'm certifiable. And besides, the subject always upsets him."

"Of your mother?" Reid asked.

"Well, yes, but mostly of Missy."

"Your sister? What about Missy?"

"In my dream, my mother was talking, barely. Her voice was odd, like an old woman who had smoked too many cigarettes, and her laugh sounded closer to that of a witch.

She was...I think she was dying." I took a deep breath and tried to push the dream's images away, those of the nearly skeletal woman with faded red hair that could be mine in time. "Anyway, in my dream, she spoke and said it was important for me to know that they forced her to tell."

"Who forced her? To tell what?" Reid asked.

I shrugged. "I don't know. She said *they* know so I needed to know."

Reid reached for my hand. "You're shaking."

"I-I..." I squeezed his hand and cuddled toward his warmth. "It's so strange. The whole thing felt real, but I know it wasn't."

"What did she want you to know?"

"First, she apologized for all the mistakes she'd made." I leaned away, still holding his hand and caught Reid's gaze. "See, like Laurel said, my mind is on some crazy-ass drugs. The only thing Nancy Pierce was ever sorry about was having three kids to take care of."

"Is that what she wanted you to know?"

"Not really." I lay back, pulling our linked hands over me. "Here's the really crazy part: she said she'd lied."

"About?"

"If it were real, the list would be long. In my dream, she said Missy was never kidnapped."

My husband's body tensed beside me. "What?"

I nodded. "Yes, I told you...crazy."

"What happened to your sister if she wasn't kidnapped?"

His voice deepened as he lifted his head to see me better. "Oh God, she didn't...your mother didn't...hurt her, did she?"

"No. She said he offered her money so she agreed to sell her."

"What the fuck? Your mother sold your sister?"

"In my dream," I reminded him. "And here's the kicker. It wasn't, like, to a sicko as we'd feared. My mom said she sold Missy to her biological father."

Reid's eyes opened wide.

I laid my head back on the pillow. "I told you, it's nuts. Even Nancy wasn't that big of a bitch to sell her own daughter." I let out a long sigh and rolled toward my husband. "Thank you for listening. I feel better just saying it. Now, I hear how absurd it is. I mean, if that were true, that would mean that Mace's and my sister wasn't taken into the Sparrow or McFadden sex rings. She grew up with her biological father." I shrugged. "Hell, Mace and I don't know the identity of the men who donated sperm to make us much less the one who contributed to her DNA." After a yawn, I scoffed and kissed Reid's cheek. "Good night. I'm going to try to sleep."

As slumber began to overtake me, I heard Reid mutter, "Well, fuck."

Thank you for reading *DUSK*...find out what happens next in *DARK*.
Pre-order your copy today by clicking on the link.

Thank you for reading *DUSK*, book #1 of Reid and Lorna's story, *Dangerous Web*. If you enjoyed *DUSK* and want to know more about our other Sparrow men, *Web of Sin*, Sterling and Araneae's story is complete with *SECRETS* (FREE), *LIES*, and *PROMISES*.

Mason and Laurel's story is also complete in *Tangled Web*, with *TWISTED, OBSESSED*, and *BOUND*.

And Patrick and Madeline's story is complete in *Web of Desire*, with *SPARK, FLAME*, and *ASHES*.

It's time to binge Sparrow Webs!

ACKNOWLEDGMENTS

A special thank you to my beta readers: Sherry, Angie, Val, Ilona, and Mr.Jeff, my editor, Lisa Aurello, my sensitivity readers, Renita McKinney and Yulanda Bolton, and my friend and publicist, Dani Sanchez of Wildfire Marketing for their dedication to my Sparrow Web world, the array of characters, and to making Reid and Lorna's story the best it can be.

You are all greatly appreciated. Please know, I couldn't do this without you.

Thank you.

WHAT TO DO NOW

LEND IT: Did you enjoy DUSK? Do you have a friend who'd enjoy DUSK? DUSK may be lent one time. Sharing is caring!

RECOMMEND IT: Do you have multiple friends who'd enjoy my dark romance with twists and turns and an all new sexy and infuriating anti-hero? Tell them about it! Call, text, post, tweet...your recommendation is the nicest gift you can give to an author!

REVIEW IT: Tell the world. Please go to the retailer where you purchased this book, as well as Goodreads, and write a review. Please share your thoughts about DUSK on:

*Amazon, DUSK Customer Reviews

*Barnes & Noble, DUSK, Customer Reviews

*iBooks, DUSK Customer Reviews

* BookBub, DUSK Customer Reviews

*Goodreads.com/Aleatha Romig

BOOKS BY NEW YORK TIMES BESTSELLING AUTHOR
ALEATHA ROMIG

NEW STORY COMING:

DEVIL'S DEAL

Coming May 2121

THE SPARROW WEBS:

DANGEROUS WEB:

DUSK

Releasing Nov, 2020

DARK

Releasing 2021

DAWN

Releasing 2021

WEB OF DESIRE:

SPARK

Released Jan. 14, 2020

FLAME

Released February 25, 2020

ASHES

Released April 7, 2020

TANGLED WEB:

TWISTED

Released May, 2019

OBSESSED

Released July, 2019

BOUND

Released August, 2019

WEB OF SIN:

SECRETS

Released October, 2018

LIES

Released December, 2018

PROMISES

Released January, 2019

THE INFIDELITY SERIES:

BETRAYAL

Book #1

Released October 2015

CUNNING

Book #2

Released January 2016

DECEPTION

Book #3

Released May 2016

ENTRAPMENT

Book #4

Released September 2016

FIDELITY

Book #5

Released January 2017

THE CONSEQUENCES SERIES:

CONSEQUENCES

(Book #1)

Released August 2011

TRUTH

(Book #2)

Released October 2012

CONVICTED

(Book #3)

Released October 2013

REVEALED

(Book #4)

Previously titled: Behind His Eyes Convicted: The Missing Years

Re-released June 2014

BEYOND THE CONSEQUENCES

(Book #5)

Released January 2015

RIPPLES

Released October 2017

CONSEQUENCES COMPANION READS:

BEHIND HIS EYES-CONSEQUENCES

Released January 2014

BEHIND HIS EYES-TRUTH

Released March 2014

STAND ALONE MAFIA THRILLER:

PRICE OF HONOR

Available Now

THE LIGHT DUET:

Published through Thomas and Mercer Amazon exclusive

INTO THE LIGHT

Released June, 2016

AWAY FROM THE DARK

Released October, 2016

TALES FROM THE DARK SIDE SERIES:

INSIDIOUS

(All books in this series are stand-alone erotic thrillers)

Released October 2014

ALEATHA'S LIGHTER ONES:

PLUS ONE

Stand-alone fun, sexy romance

May 2017

ANOTHER ONE

Stand-alone fun, sexy romance

May 2018

ONE NIGHT

Stand-alone, sexy contemporary romance

September 2017

A SECRET ONE

April 2018

INDULGENCE SERIES:

UNEXPECTED

Released August, 2018

UNCONVENTIONAL

Released January, 2018

UNFORGETTABLE

Released October, 2019

UNDENIABLE

Coming late summer 2020

ABOUT THE AUTHOR

Aleatha Romig is a New York Times, Wall Street Journal, and USA Today bestselling author who lives in Indiana, USA. She has raised three children with her high school sweetheart and husband of over thirty years. Before she became a full-time author, she worked days as a dental hygienist and spent her nights writing. Now, when she's not imagining mind-blowing twists and turns, she likes to spend her time with her family and friends. Her other pastimes include reading and creating heroes/anti-heroes who haunt your dreams!

Aleatha impresses with her versatility in writing. She released her first novel, CONSEQUENCES, in August of 2011. CONSEQUENCES, a dark romance, became a bestselling series with five novels and two companions released from 2011 through 2015. The compelling and epic story of Anthony and Claire Rawlings has graced more than half a million e-readers. Her first stand-alone smart, sexy thriller INSIDIOUS was next. Then Aleatha released the five-novel INFIDELITY series, a romantic suspense saga, that took the reading world by storm, the final book landing on three of the top bestseller lists. She ventured into traditional publishing with Thomas and Mercer. Her books INTO THE LIGHT and AWAY FROM THE DARK were published through this mystery/thriller publisher in 2016. In the spring of 2017, Aleatha again ventured into a different genre with her first fun and sexy stand-alone romantic comedy with the USA Today bestseller PLUS ONE. She continued with ONE NIGHT and ANOTHER ONE. If you like fun, sexy, novellas that make your heart pound, try her UNCONVENTIONAL and UNEXPECTED. In 2018 Aleatha returned to her dark romance roots with SPARROW WEBS.

Aleatha is a "Published Author's Network" member of the Romance Writers of America and PEN America. She is represented by Kevan Lyon of Marsal Lyon Literary Agency and Dani Sanchez with Wildfire Marketing.

facebook.com/aleatharomig
twitter.com/aleatharomig
instagram.com/aleatharomig

Made in the USA
Columbia, SC
20 July 2022

63622180R00167